MARVEL CINEMATIC UNIVERSE
PHASE TWO

MARVEL

CAPTAIN AMERICA
THE WINTER SOLDIER

MARVEL CINEMATIC UNIVERSE
PHASE TWO

MARVEL

CAPTAIN AMERICA
THE WINTER SOLDIER

Adapted by ALEX IRVINE

Based on the Screenplay by CHRISTOPHER MARKUS
and STEPHEN McFEELY

Produced by KEVIN FEIGE, P.G.A.

Directed by ANTHONY RUSSO and JOE RUSSO

Ⓛ Ⓑ

LITTLE, BROWN AND COMPANY
New York   Boston

marvelkids.com

© 2016 by MARVEL

Excerpt from *Phase Two: Avengers: Age of Ultron* copyright © 2015 by Marvel

Little, Brown and Company

Hachette Book Group
1290 Avenue of the Americas, New York, NY 10104
Visit us at lb-kids.com

Little, Brown and Company is a division of Hachette Book Group, Inc.
The Little, Brown name and logo are trademarks of Hachette Book Group, Inc.

The publisher is not responsible for websites (or their content)
that are not owned by the publisher.

First Edition: February 2016

ISBN: 978-0-316-25678-0

10 9 8 7 6 5 4 3 2 1

RRD-C

Printed in the United States of America

CHAPTER 1

It was a fine cool morning to be jogging on the National Mall in Washington, DC. Sam Wilson planned to put in his miles and then he had to get to work at the VA rehab facility. He liked running on mornings like these, before the heat settled in and DC turned into a steam bath. He wasn't thinking about much, just enjoying the groove of the run, the feeling of his body getting loose. He heard a voice from behind him. "On your left."

Sam nodded. It was standard runner's courtesy to let someone know when you were going to pass them on a path. But the other guy was moving fast. Really fast.

Almost at a sprint. He shot ahead of Sam and made a turn, disappearing behind the Lincoln Memorial. If he kept up that pace, he wasn't going to get very far. Sam decided he must be doing some kind of interval workout. Sprints, then walks. Something like that.

Sam's standard loop around the National Mall was almost exactly four miles. The first time he saw the fast guy was about a mile and a half into it. Then, before he reached the three-mile mark, he heard it again. "On your left."

There he went again. "Uh-huh. On my left. Got it," Sam said. He considered himself to be in pretty good shape, but this guy was Olympic level. Unless he was catching a ride or something. He watched the other runner go, and picked up his own pace. A little competition was good. He could go faster and he didn't like having other runners show him up. His lungs started to burn and he could feel the muscles in his legs burn, too. This wasn't just a regular jog anymore.

When he was a few hundred yards short of the complete loop, he heard footsteps again. "Don't say it. Don't you say it," he said, trying to go faster, but he was pretty worn out.

"On your left." The other runner went by at the same robotic near-sprint.

"Come on!" Sam said. He started to sprint, too. When he got to the four-mile mark, he staggered off the path and sat down by a tree, panting. It had been a long time since he'd run that hard.

The other guy had stopped, too. He strolled back over to Sam, barely out of breath. Now that Sam saw his face, he started to figure out how the guy had kept up that crazy pace. "Need a medic?" he asked Sam.

"I need a new set of lungs," Sam said, half-serious.

"Dude, you just ran, like, thirteen miles in thirty minutes."

"I guess I got a late start."

"Really? You should be ashamed of yourself. You should take another lap. Did you just take it? I assume you just took it." Sam laughed at himself.

"What unit you with?" Mister Fast asked.

"Fifty-Eighth Pararescue. But now I'm working down at the VA." Sam got to his feet and extended a hand. "Sam Wilson."

"Steve Rogers."

"I kind of put that together." Sam couldn't believe he was talking to Captain America. "Must have freaked you out, coming home after the whole defrosting thing."

"It takes some getting used to. It's good to meet you, Sam." Captain America turned to go.

Sam was a little bit starstruck and a little bit curious. He also felt like maybe he'd put his foot in his mouth by bringing up the defrosting thing. "It's your bed, right?" he called out.

Steve turned back. "What's that?"

"Your bed, it's too soft. When I was over there, I'd sleep on the ground, use rocks for pillows like a caveman. Now I'm home, lying in my bed, and it's like..."

"Lying on a marshmallow," Steve finished.

"Feel like I'm gonna sink right to the floor," Sam said.

Steve nodded. "How long?"

"Two tours. You must miss the good old days, huh?"

Steve thought about it. "Well, things aren't so bad. Food's a lot better. We used to boil everything. No polio is good. Internet, so helpful. I've been reading that a lot, trying to catch up."

I bet you spend a lot of time trying to catch up, Sam thought. He had an idea. "Marvin Gaye, 1972, *Trouble Man* soundtrack," he said. "Everything you missed jammed into one album."

"I'll put it on the list." Sam saw him write it down in a little spiral notebook. Then Steve's phone chirped. He looked at his screen and said, "All right, Sam, duty calls."

"Thanks for the run."

"If that's what you want to call running," Steve joked.

Sam laughed. "Oh, that's how it is?"

"Oh, that's how it is."

"Okay." Sam waved. "Any time you want to stop by the VA, make me look awesome in front of the girl at the front desk, just let me know."

"I'll keep it in mind," Steve said with a grin.

With a rev of its overpowered engine, a black sports car pulled up to the curb nearby. The driver was a young red-headed woman Sam recognized immediately: Agent Natasha Romanoff of S.H.I.E.L.D. *Holy smokes*, he thought. *This sure is better than bumping into senators while you're trying to cross Pennsylvania Avenue.* "Hey, fellas," Romanoff said. "Either one of you know where the Smithsonian is? I'm here to pick up a fossil."

Steve glanced over at Sam as he walked to the car. He figured Sam would be checking Natasha out and he was right. She was hard to ignore. "That's hilarious."

As he got in the car, he saw that Natasha was also checking Sam out. "How you doing?" Sam said.

She gave him a little smile. "Hey."

Steve grinned at him. "Can't run everywhere," he said.

As the car squealed away into traffic, Sam Wilson said to himself, "No, you can't."

Man, he thought. *I just met two of the Avengers.*

But he still had to go home, get a shower, and get to work. Life went on.

CHAPTER 2

S.T.R.I.K.E. team leader Brock Rumlow briefed Cap and Natasha as they flew in a Quinjet over the Indian Ocean. "Target is a mobile satellite launch platform, the *Lemurian Star*. They were sending up their last payload when pirates took them, ninety-three minutes ago." Rumlow was working on a touch screen in the Quinjet's passenger compartment. He showed the ship and then its location on the map, close to the Indian coast.

"Any demands?" Steve asked.

"Billion and a half."

"Why so steep?"

"Because it's S.H.I.E.L.D.'s," Rumlow said.

That changed things. This wasn't an ordinary hijacking. "So it's not off course," Steve said. "It's trespassing."

"I'm sure they have a good reason," Natasha said.

"You know, I'm getting a little tired of being Fury's janitor."

"Relax. It's not that complicated."

"How many pirates?" Steve asked Rumlow.

"Twenty-five. Top mercs led by this guy." Rumlow pulled up a dossier on the screen. "Georges Batroc. Ex-DGSE, Action Division. He's at the top of Interpol's Red Notice. Before the French demobilized him, he had thirty-six kill missions. This guy's got a rep for maximum casualties."

"Hostages?"

"Oh, mostly techs. One officer. Jasper Sitwell." A photo of Sitwell appeared on the screen. "They're in the galley."

Steve knew Jasper Sitwell. He wasn't usually in the field. "What's Sitwell doing on a launch ship?" he wondered aloud.

Steve considered the layout of the ship and the location of the galley where the hostages were. Everything seemed pretty straightforward. "All right, I'm gonna sweep the deck and find Batroc. Nat, you kill the engines and wait for instructions." He looked at Rumlow. "Rumlow, you sweep aft, find the hostages, get them to the life-pods, get them out. Let's move."

"S.T.R.I.K.E., you heard the cap," Rumlow said. "Gear up."

"Secure channel seven," Steve said into his wrist mic, testing the frequency he would use on the operation.

"Seven secure," Natasha echoed. "Did you do anything fun Saturday night?"

"Well, all the guys from my barbershop quartet are dead, so, no, not really."

"Coming up on the drop zone, Cap," Rumlow said from up front.

"You know, if you ask Kristen from Statistics out, she'd probably say yes," Natasha said. Lately she'd started a campaign to get him to date more. Or at all.

Steve knew she was right about Kristen from Statistics. "That's why I don't ask," he said. The Quinjet's rear ramp opened up, exposing a stormy night sky.

"Too shy, or too scared?"

"Too busy!" Cap jumped out the back of the plane.

Rumlow and his second-in-command, Jack Rollins, saw Cap jump. "Was he wearing a parachute?" Rollins asked.

"No," Rumlow said with an admiring smile. "No, he wasn't."

CHAPTER 3

Steve fell through the stormy night toward the hijacked ship, then veered away and somersaulted at the last moment so he hit the water feet-first. The icy shock up his legs felt good, like the first little jab to the face when you were sparring. It woke you up, let you know it was time to focus on the mission. He'd fallen from a few hundred feet, and went pretty deep. He surfaced, climbed the side of the ship's hull, vaulted the railing, and then landed softly behind an unsuspecting mercenary on patrol.

Steve grabbed him from behind and covered his mouth, putting him in a chokehold until he was unconscious.

Then he lowered the mercenary to the deck. He needed to keep up the element of surprise as long as he could.

He went counterclockwise around the deck of the ship, taking out the mercenaries as he found them. He used exactly as much force as was necessary to stop them from sounding the alarm.

Everything went fine right up until he had made an almost complete circuit of the ship. Then, just as he began to turn into the middle of the deck to get inside and head for the galley, he skidded to a halt. One of the mercenaries had him covered with an automatic rifle. "Don't move!" he shouted.

Steve froze. Out of the corner of his eye, he saw another armed mercenary. They had overlapping fields of fire and he had no place to run. He could probably take them down, but he was going to lose some blood doing it.

Then there was a soft pop and the nearest mercenary collapsed. Before he even hit the deck, the second man also fell. A moment later Brock Rumlow dropped out of the sky, parachute trailing behind him over the deck. He held the rifle he'd used to drop the two mercenaries. *Good shooting*, Steve thought. It wasn't easy to be accurate when you were hanging from a parachute on a windy night and shooting at a moving target on the deck of a ship, which was also moving. Rumlow was among S.H.I.E.L.D.'s best.

"Thanks," Cap said.

"Yeah," Rumlow said with a grin. "You seemed pretty helpless without me."

Natasha and the rest of the team dropped around them and together they all started off to the next mission objective: Find Sitwell and also find Georges Batroc. "What about the nurse who lives across the hall from you?" Natasha asked Steve as they walked. "She seems kind of nice."

Her name was Kate, and Natasha was right. She was nice. Steve appreciated what Natasha was trying to do, but his mind wasn't on romance right then. "Secure the engine room, then find me a date."

"I'm multitasking," she said, and vaulted a railing before dropping down to the lower deck, where the engine room was.

CHAPTER 4

In the galley, the mercenaries were getting impatient. "I told Batroc," one of them said in French, "if we want to make S.H.I.E.L.D. pay us, start sending them bodies now!" He walked up and down the row of hostages. They were all sitting on the floor, hands and feet tied. "I have a bullet for someone.... You want a bullet in your head?" He kicked Jasper Sitwell's foot. "Move that foot—you want a bullet in the head?"

Sitwell just looked at him. He knew S.H.I.E.L.D. would have launched a rescue mission. It was only a matter of time.

Steve got to the lower level of the ship's bridge tower and shot a small, sticky disk up to the bridge window. The disk contained a microphone that let him in on what the mercenaries were saying. "I don't like waiting," one of them was complaining in French.

"Call Durand," another said. "I want this ship ready to move when the ransom comes."

There was a pause, and Steve heard the first mercenary say, "Start the engines." Then he hung up the phone.

Down in the engine room, the mercenary who had taken the call turned to get the engines started. He froze when he saw Natasha Romanoff, smiling at him. "Hey, sailor," she said.

In the galley, the restless mercenary got sick of shouting at the hostages. "All right, I've waited long enough," he announced, and pounded on the door. "Hey! Find Batroc. If I don't hear anything in two minutes, I start killing them!"

"I'll find him," the mercenary outside called back.

But when he turned around, he walked right into Brock Rumlow's Taser. He went down without a sound. The rest of the S.T.R.I.K.E. team waited with Rumlow for the order to go in.

Outside, Cap was watching the bridge and still listening in. He knew Batroc was up there when one of the mercenaries said, "Radio silence from S.H.I.E.L.D., Batroc."

"S.T.R.I.K.E. in position," Rumlow reported.

It was time to go in. "Natasha, what's your status?" She didn't answer. "Status, Natasha."

"Hang on!" Natasha snapped. She was a little busy with the last three mercenaries in the engine room area. She took them out with a combination of unarmed strikes and electrical jolts from the stingers built into the wrists of her uniform. Then she got back to Steve. "Engine room secure."

Inside the galley, the mercenaries got ready as the two minutes ran out. "Time is up," the leader said. "Who dies first?" He pointed at a random agent. "You!"

Then there was a series of sharp cracks as the galley's windows shattered by S.T.R.I.K.E. snipers hanging outside. The mercenaries all dropped. A split second later, the galley door blew off its hinges, and with a single shot, Brock Rumlow took out the leader who had started the two-minute countdown.

He fell right in front of Jasper Sitwell, who looked at him and said, "I told you. S.H.I.E.L.D. doesn't negotiate."

CHAPTER 5

On the bridge, the mercenary with Batroc looked at his phone. "The line just went dead. I've lost contact with them...."

Captain America's shield shattered through the window. Batroc dodged the shield with extraordinary reflexes and it knocked out the other mercenary instead and got lodged in the wall. Steve vaulted through the broken window into the bridge compartment.

While Cap was regaining his balance, Batroc kicked out from his hiding place behind a row of navigation terminals and ran. Cap pulled his shield out of the wall and followed, hurtling down a stairwell and coming out onto the main deck.

"Hostages en route to extraction. Romanoff missed the rendezvous point, Captain," Rumlow said in his ear. "Hostiles are still in play."

"Natasha, Batroc's on the move," Steve said into the wrist comm. "Circle back to Rumlow and protect the hostages." She didn't answer. "Natasha," he said again.

Still no answer.

Batroc took advantage of Cap's distraction, jumping out of the shadows and nailing him with a series of leaping and spinning kicks. Cap absorbed most of them with his shield, but Batroc seemed quicker than any normal man. He kept coming, and he dodged Cap's counterattacks. After their first round, Batroc did a back handspring away, and in French said, "I thought you were more than just a shield."

Okay, Steve thought. *Fair enough.*

He attached the shield to its magnetic clamp on his back. Then he took off his mask. "Let's see," he said, also in French.

The second round was close and short. Steve went after Batroc, knowing he'd have to take a punch to get in close without his shield. That was all right. He got into grappling distance with Batroc and pounded him to the ground. Batroc kicked loose and got up. Steve charged him. They crashed through a door and slammed to the floor inside a room full of computers. With one last punch, Steve knocked Batroc out cold.

"Well, this is awkward," Natasha said.

Steve looked up. She was at one of the terminals. Had she been here the whole time, not answering his calls and missing the S.T.R.I.K.E. rendezvous? "What are you doing?" he asked.

"Backing up the hard drive. It's a good habit to get into."

"Rumlow needed your help. What are you doing here?" He looked at the computer screen and saw the names of the files she was downloading. "You're saving S.H.I.E.L.D. intel."

"Whatever I can get my hands on."

She had gone completely off mission and Steve didn't like it. "Our mission is to rescue hostages."

"No, that's your mission, and you've done it beautifully," she said. She finished the download and popped a USB drive out of its socket.

Steve was starting to get angry, not just because she had gone missing in the middle of a mission but because she didn't seem to care. "You just jeopardized this whole operation," he said.

Natasha stuck the USB drive in her belt. "I think that's overstating things."

There was motion in the corner of the room. Steve and Natasha looked up to see Batroc throwing a grenade at them while he ran out the door. Apparently he wasn't as unconscious as Steve had thought.

He grabbed Natasha and they dove out of the room onto the deck as the grenade blew out the windows behind them. Smoke and fire billowed over their heads. Both of them were stung by flying debris, but neither was seriously hurt.

"Okay," Natasha said while the smoke started to clear. "That one's on me."

Steve was still angry, and he didn't appreciate the way she wasn't taking him seriously. "You're right," he said, and got up to look for Batroc—but the mercenary was long gone.

CHAPTER 6

At the Triskelion, S.H.I.E.L.D.'s new headquarters, Steve strode into Nick Fury's office. He was still angry about what Natasha had done, and he was also angry at Nick Fury for misleading the team about the nature of the mission on the *Lemurian Star*.

"You just can't stop yourself from lying, can you?" he said as he came in.

"I didn't lie," Fury said. He was sitting at his desk looking out the window, away from Steve. "Agent Romanoff had a different mission than yours."

"Which you didn't feel obliged to share."

"I'm not obliged to do anything," Fury said.

This was true and Steve knew it, but he didn't have to like it. "Those hostages could have died, Nick."

"I sent the greatest soldier in history to make sure that didn't happen," Fury said, turning to face Steve as Steve reached the desk.

Steve wasn't in the mood to be flattered. "Soldiers trust each other. That's what makes it an army. Not a bunch of guys running around shooting guns."

"Last time I trusted someone, I lost an eye." Fury stood and leaned over his desk. He wasn't backing down. "Look, I didn't want you doing anything you weren't comfortable with. Agent Romanoff is comfortable with everything."

Steve didn't back down, either. "I can't lead a mission when the people I'm leading have missions of their own," he said.

"It's called compartmentalization," Fury said. "Nobody spills the secrets, because nobody knows them all."

"Except you."

Fury appeared to change his mind about something. "You're wrong about me," he said. "I do share. I'm nice like that."

He walked toward the elevator and Steve followed him. "Insight bay," Fury said as they got in.

The elevator's facial recognition software identified Steve immediately. "Captain Rogers does not have clearance for Project Insight," a computer voice said.

"Director override. Fury, Nicholas J."

"Confirmed."

"You know, they used to play music," Steve said as they went down. The elevator was glass and built on the outside of the Triskelion tower, and offered a great view of Washington, DC.

"Yeah. My grandfather operated one of these things for forty years. Granddad worked in a nice building. Got good tips. He'd walk home every night, a roll of ones stuffed in his lunch bag. He'd say hi. People would say hi back. Time went on, the neighborhood got rougher. He'd say hi. They'd say, 'Keep on steppin'.' Granddad got to gripping that lunch bag a little tighter."

Steve knew plenty of neighborhoods like that. "Did he ever get mugged?"

"Every week some punk would say, 'What's in the bag?'"

Everything got dark except for the elevator's operating lights as they descended below ground level. "What would he do?" Steve asked.

"He'd show them. Bunch of crumpled ones and a loaded

twenty-two Magnum. Yeah, Granddad loved people. But he didn't trust them very much."

I guess not, Steve thought. *Neither does his grandson.*

Fury walked to the other side of the elevator as the light changed. There was a glow coming from outside. Steve turned to see a vast hangar, at least a mile across, built out under the river. It was so big that it had its own roads, with trucks and cargo carts driving materials and supplies in every direction. Thousands of people were working there, on and around one of the most amazing things Steve had ever seen.

CHAPTER 7

There were three Helicarriers lined up in the hangar. They all had rows of swiveling turrets on the sides of their hulls and along their flight decks. Also on their flight decks were lines of Quinjets. Every one of them looked like it could take on an entire navy all by itself... and win.

"Yeah, I know," Fury said, seeing the astonished look on Steve's face. "They're a little bit bigger than a twenty-two."

When they got out on the floor, Fury gave Steve the rundown on what S.H.I.E.L.D. had been up to. "This is

Project Insight. Three next-generation Helicarriers synced to a network of targeting satellites."

Steve put two and two together. "Launched from the *Lemurian Star.*"

"Once we get them in the air, they never need to come down. Continuous suborbital flight, courtesy of our new repulsor engines."

"Stark?" Steve wasn't surprised to hear that Tony was involved. To him, these giant new Helicarriers would be toys. To Steve, they looked like something else entirely, and he didn't like it very much.

"He had a few suggestions once he got an up-close look at our old turbines," Fury said. They walked underneath one of the Helicarriers. The bottom of its hull bristled with gun turrets. Behind them was a huge glass bubble with satellite and radar dishes on its inner surface. "These new long-range precision guns can eliminate a thousand hostiles a minute. The satellites can read a terrorist's DNA before he steps outside his spider hole. We're gonna neutralize a lot of threats before they even happen."

Steve had seen enough. He had to speak up. It was disturbing to think a project this big had happened without him knowing about it, but now that he heard Fury's reasons, he liked it even less. "Thought the punishment usually came after the crime," he said.

Deadly serious, Fury answered, "We can't afford to wait that long."

"Who's we?"

"After New York, I convinced the World Security Council we needed a quantum surge in threat analysis. For once, we're way ahead of the curve."

"By holding a gun to everyone on Earth and calling it protection."

"You know, I read those SSR files," Fury said. "'Greatest Generation'? You guys did some nasty stuff."

This was true. "Yeah, we compromised," Steve admitted. "Sometimes in ways that made us not sleep so well. But we did it so that people could be free." He looked up at the Helicarrier again, and imagined what it would be like if he was a civilian seeing it in the sky. "This isn't freedom. This is fear."

"S.H.I.E.L.D. takes the world as it is, not as we'd like it to be. And it's getting near past time for you to get with that program, Cap."

Steve couldn't believe Fury had bought into this idea. The whole point of the Avengers was the idea that you fought for the world you wanted. A better world. You didn't just give up and stop trying to believe in what was right. Having bigger guns wasn't going to make the world a safer place, because how did you know you could trust the people aiming the guns?

"Don't hold your breath," Steve said, and walked away.

CHAPTER 8

Steve got on his motorcycle and went for a ride across the river into Washington, DC. After wandering around for a while, he found himself in one of his favorite places, the Smithsonian. He loved that museum, but lately it was a little weird going there because the museum had installed an exhibit on him. Steve Rogers, walking historical relic. He felt like the world had passed him by, like everything he'd fought for had been lost because S.H.I.E.L.D. had decided that better weapons trumped better ideas.

He walked by the exhibit as the voiceover played, telling a version of his story.

"A symbol to the nation," the exhibit voiceover said as Steve walked past a giant mural of him saluting a flag. *Captain America, the Living Legend and Symbol of Courage*, read the title. "A hero to the world. The story of Captain America is one of honor, bravery, and sacrifice." Steve paused before a display showing pictures of him before and after he'd volunteered for the Super-Soldier project. "Denied enlistment due to poor health," the voiceover went on, "Steven Rogers was chosen for a program unique in the annals of American warfare. One that would transform him into the world's first Super-Soldier."

A young boy wearing a Captain America T-shirt noticed him. Recognized him. The boy's eyes popped. Steve gave him a wink and laid a finger across his lips: *Shh. Our little secret.*

I guess I really am a museum piece, he thought.

He stopped again, in front of a diorama featuring mannequins wearing the uniform of the Howling Commandos. Steve's original Captain America suit and shield were there, too. He'd been wearing them when he came out of the ice. "Battle tested, Captain America and his Howling

Commandos quickly earned their stripes. Their mission: take down Hydra, the Nazi rogue science division."

Turning, Steve saw a black-and-white picture of Bucky Barnes under the heading A FALLEN COMRADE. "Best friends since childhood, Bucky Barnes and Steven Rogers were inseparable on both schoolyard and battlefield." A film loop of Steve and Bucky played on a screen set into the display, showing him and Bucky laughing together between missions. "Barnes is the only Howling Commando to give his life in service of his country."

That's right, Steve thought. *But if Project Insight is where this country is going, what was that sacrifice worth?*

Next he went into a film room and sat in the back, watching Peggy Carter being interviewed in 1953. "That was a difficult winter. A blizzard had trapped half our battalion behind the German line. Steve, Captain Rogers, he fought his way through a Hydra blockade that had pinned our allies down for months. He saved over a thousand men. Including the man who would...who would become my husband, as it turned out."

Lucky guy, Steve thought. While he listened to Peggy's voice, he took out the compass he'd had in the war, with her picture pasted into the inside of the lid. The same picture he'd watched as the Red Skull's plane made its final dive toward the ice.

"Even after he died," Peggy said on the screen, "Steve was still changing my life."

Now that he was alive again, Steve thought, she was still changing his, too. He needed to see her again.

CHAPTER 9

Peggy was still alive but not doing very well. Her mind was foggy and she had a tendency to get lost in time. That made it difficult to talk to her sometimes, and also Steve had a hard time seeing her and remembering what he'd lost because of Hydra. He saw her anyway, and sat at her bedside in the home where she had raised her children and had the life he'd been denied.

"You should be proud of yourself, Peggy," he said, looking at old photographs on the bedside table. It was true. She'd been in on the founding of S.H.I.E.LD., conducted dozens of top-secret operations in Europe during

World War II....Most people didn't do that much in ten lifetimes.

"Mmm," she said. "I have lived a life. My only regret is that you didn't get to live yours." She saw that something was bothering him. "What is it?"

He wanted to tell her about Project Insight, but he couldn't. Even if everyone else in S.H.I.E.L.D. was spilling secrets, he wouldn't. But he wanted to say something. "For as long as I can remember, I just wanted to do what was right. I guess I'm not quite sure what that is anymore. And I thought I could throw myself back in and follow orders. Serve. It's just not the same."

"You're always so dramatic," she said. "Look, you saved the world. We rather mucked it up."

"You didn't. Knowing that you helped found S.H.I.E.L.D. is half the reason I stay."

Peggy took his hand. "Hey. The world has changed, and none of us can go back. All we can do is our best. And sometimes the best that we can do is to start over."

A coughing fit took her, and Steve got her a drink of water. Her eyes were closed as she got the coughing under control. When she opened them again, an expression of wonder came over her face. "Steve," she breathed, like he'd just come into the room.

"Yeah?"

"You're alive. You came back."

She was lost again, in the fog of age. It broke Steve's heart to see her this way, but he stuck it out. He wouldn't hurt her, even if it meant pretending something that wasn't true. "Yeah, Peggy."

"It's been so long. So long." She was crying.

"Well, I couldn't leave my best girl," Steve said. It was all he could do not to start crying himself. Instead he smiled and added, "Not when she owes me a dance."

He stayed with her until she fell asleep. When he left, he was more certain than ever about what he should do next.

CHAPTER 10

ecure office," Nick Fury said when he'd come back upstairs from the Project Insight bay. The windows' polarized and signal-baffling drapes closed them off. Other security measures he couldn't see also started up: No electronic traffic could go in or out.

He inserted the USB drive Romanoff had brought back into a terminal. "Open *Lemurian Star*'s satellite launch file."

On the big wall display near the conference table in his office, a message appeared. ACCESS DENIED. A computer voice spoke the same message aloud.

"Run decryption," he said.

"Decryption failed."

"Director override. Fury, Nicholas J."

"Override denied. All files sealed."

"On whose authority?"

"Fury, Nicholas J."

Someone had locked him out using a fake version of his own S.H.I.E.L.D. identity profile. There weren't many people who could do that...and there also weren't many people Fury could go to for help. He had known something was off about the *Lemurian Star* and its mission. That's why he had wanted Romanoff to pull the ship's data. But now he was starting to think the problem went deeper than he knew.

There was only one person he could ask about that.

He walked to the elevator, got in, and said, "World Security Council."

Alexander Pierce, current head of S.H.I.E.L.D. and liaison to the World Security Council, was dealing with a complex mess left over from the *Lemurian Star* mission. The other four councilors were present as holograms in

Pierce's top-floor conference room, which looked out over downtown Washington, DC.

"If Nick Fury thinks he can get his costumed thugs and S.T.R.I.K.E. commandos to mop up his mess, he's sadly mistaken," Councilor Rockwell said angrily. "This failure is unacceptable."

"Considering this attack took place one mile from my country's sovereign waters," added Councilor Singh, "it's a bit more than that. I move for immediate hearing."

"We don't need hearings, we need action," Councilor Hawley argued. "It's this council's duty to oversee S.H.I.E.L.D."

Councilor Yen broke in. "A breach like this raises serious questions."

"Like how did a French pirate manage to hijack a covert S.H.I.E.L.D. vessel in broad daylight?" Rockwell demanded.

"For the record, Councilman, he's Algerian," Pierce said. He was getting tired of their grandstanding. "I can draw a map if it'd help."

Rockwell didn't react to Pierce's joke. "I appreciate your wit, Secretary Pierce. But this council takes things like international piracy fairly seriously."

"Really? I don't," Pierce said. Powell had given him

an opening and he was taking it. "I don't care about one boat, I care about the fleet. If this council is going to fall to rancor every time someone pushes us on the playing field, maybe we need someone to oversee us."

Yen tried to ease the tension. "Mr. Secretary, nobody is suggesting…"

One of Pierce's aides came in and told him that Nick Fury was in his office, and not in a mood to wait. "Excuse me," he said to the council. They could talk about him while he was gone.

"More trouble, Mr. Secretary?" Powell asked.

"Depends on your definition," Pierce said as he left the conference room. His aide shut the door behind them and Pierce greeted Fury with a smile and a handshake. "I work forty floors away and it takes a hijacking for you to visit?"

"A nuclear war would do it, too." Fury looked through the window into the conference room, where he could see but not hear the hologram council. "You busy in there?"

Pierce shrugged. He was a veteran of these kinds of battles. "Nothing some earmarks can't fix."

"I'm here to ask a favor. I want you to call for a vote. Project Insight has to be delayed."

"Nick, that's not a favor, that's a subcommittee hearing," Pierce said. "A long one." Project Insight was ready to launch. The council wanted to see it happen, and they wanted to see it happen now. Slowing it down wouldn't be easy.

"It could be nothing," Fury said. "It probably is nothing. I just need time to make sure it's nothing."

"But if it's something?" Pierce was curious to see how much he could get out of Fury.

"Then we'll both be glad those Helicarriers aren't in the air," Fury said quietly. Then he waited.

They'd known each other for a long time, and both men knew that if Fury was asking a favor the issue was important. "Fine," Pierce said. "But you got to get Iron Man to stop by my niece's birthday party."

"Thank you, sir." They shook hands again.

"And not just a flyby," Pierce said, making sure Fury understood how big a favor he was asking. "He's got to mingle."

CHAPTER 11

Steve thought he would stop by the VA and follow up on seeing what he could do to help Sam impress his friends. He needed to connect with some regular people. All he ever saw were S.H.I.E.L.D. colleagues and people from his past. Seeing the film of Bucky and Peggy had made him sad. Seeing Peggy in person had made him even sadder. He was feeling adrift, and Sam had reached out. That meant something to Steve, so he went looking for Sam and found him running a support group for vets working through post-traumatic stress.

"The thing is, I think it's getting worse," a woman was

saying as Steve got to the doorway of the meeting room. He saw Sam standing in front of a group of people in rows of folding chairs. Sam was listening as the woman continued her story. "A cop pulled me over last week. He thought I was drunk. I swerved to miss a plastic bag. I thought it was an IED."

Steve leaned against the doorway, not wanting to intrude.

"Some stuff you leave there," Sam said. "Other stuff you bring back. It's our job to figure out how to carry it. Is it gonna be in a big suitcase, or in a little man purse? It's up to you."

He wrapped up the meeting, and as the group dispersed, he walked up to Steve. "Look who it is—the Running Man."

Steve nodded at the now-empty room. "Caught the last few minutes. It's pretty intense."

"Yeah, brother, we all got the same problems. Guilt, regret…" Sam trailed off.

"You lose someone?"

Sam nodded. "My wingman, Riley. Flying a night mission. Standard PJ rescue op. Nothing we hadn't done a thousand times before. Until an RPG knocked Riley out of the sky. Nothing I could do. It's like I was up there just to watch."

"I'm sorry," Steve said. It was all you could say.

"After that, I had a really hard time finding a reason for being over there, you know?"

Steve looked around at the meeting room, the files Sam was gathering…all the regular stuff for a regular job. "But you're happy now, back in the world?"

"The number of people giving me orders is down to about zero. So, yeah." Sam grinned. "Are you thinking about getting out?"

"No," Steve said. Then he corrected himself. "I don't know. To be honest, I don't know what I would do with myself if I did."

"Ultimate Fighting?" They both chuckled. "Just a great idea off the top of my head. Seriously, you could do whatever you want to do. What makes you happy?"

That was the problem, Steve thought. He didn't know.

CHAPTER 12

Fury drove through DC. He had a lot on his mind. The *Lemurian Star* operation was looking more and more like he was on to something, but he wasn't sure what, because he couldn't access the data on the USB drive. Being locked out of his own security clearance was a bad sign. Someone who didn't belong had gotten into S.H.I.E.L.D. The question was who.

"Activating communications encryption protocol," the car computer said.

"Open secure line 0405."

"Confirmed."

Maria Hill's face appeared on a holographic display in the upper left corner of his windshield. "This is Hill."

"I need you here in DC," Fury said, getting right to the point. "Deep shadow conditions."

"Give me four hours."

"You have three. Over." He ended the call and stopped at the next light.

A police car pulled up next to him. The two cops inside were both staring at Fury, their expressions hostile and their eyes hidden by mirrored sunglasses.

Fury didn't have time for hassles from cops. "Want to see my lease?" he said.

The light changed and the cop car started to pull ahead of him. Fury pulled out into the intersection—and a car slammed into him from the left. His airbag deployed as a second car rear-ended him. The cop car ahead squealed into reverse, crashing into the front of his car. Dazed, he barely noticed the fourth car hit on the passenger side. He was trapped...and he had a feeling he wasn't dealing with actual cops.

His car's dashboard display was cutting-edge Stark technology, and it had already done a medical scan. An image of his body, with the left arm blinking red, appeared on a screen. "Fracture detected. Recommend anesthetic injection," the system reported.

Fury leaned over and punched a syringe from the glove compartment into his arm. Black SUVs skidded to a halt all around him and armed men deployed, all of them pointing guns at Fury's car.

"DC Metro Police dispatch shows no units in this area," the car said.

Just as Fury had figured. This was an assassination attempt. The infiltration of S.H.I.E.L.D. had gone further than he'd thought. It wasn't just spying. It was a hostile takeover.

"Get me out of here," he said. Outside, the fake cops opened fire. Fury's car was armored, and the windows were bulletproof, but they wouldn't stand up forever.

"Propulsion systems offline," the car said.

"Then reboot!"

The windows were starred with bullet impacts, but the car could hold out against small-arms fire for a long time. Fury's mind raced. He'd been in plenty of tough spots. How would he get out of this one?

The attackers outside stopped firing as four of them hauled a pneumatic battering ram from the back of a van.

They set it up right next to Fury's window. "Warning. Window integrity compromised."

"You think?" He scooted over into the passenger seat. "How long to propulsion?"

"Calculating."

When the battering ram slammed into the window, the whole car rocked up on two wheels before bouncing back down. "Window integrity thirty-one percent," the car said. "Deploying countermeasures."

"Hold that order!" He was starting to come up with a plan, but it would depend on perfect timing.

WHAM! The battering ram rocked the car again. "Window integrity nineteen percent. Offensive measures advised."

"Wait!"

A third blow from the battering ram left the window completely spiderwebbed with cracks. "Window integrity one percent," the car said.

"Now!" Fury shouted.

CHAPTER 13

From the console between the front seats of Fury's car, a small machine gun turret unfolded. Before the battering ram could hit him again, Fury gripped the stock and unloaded on the team operating it. The window, so close to breaking, did nothing to stop the bullets.

After taking out the battering ram team, he racked the grenade launcher barrel on the turret and fired into the back of the SUV. It blew up in a huge fireball, catching two of the nearby cars on fire, too.

"Propulsion systems now online," the car said.

"Full acceleration! Now!" He kept firing as his car

slammed the police cars out of the way and squealed down the street. Once he was clear of the initial ambush, he said, "Initiate vertical takeoff!"

"Flight systems damaged."

"Then activate guidance cameras!"

Rear-facing camera views showed up on his windshield. Fury cried out in pain from his broken arm as he got back in the driver's seat. "Give me the wheel!"

He had a little head start, but the assassins were on his tail. He had to alert Maria Hill and get some emergency plans in place for the team. "Get me Agent Hill."

"Communications array damaged."

"Well, what's not damaged?" he shouted in frustration.

"Air-conditioning is fully operational." The car computer clearly didn't understand humor or sarcasm.

"Traffic ahead."

"Give me an alternate route."

"Traffic alert on Roosevelt Bridge. All vehicles stopped. Seventeenth Avenue clear in three blocks, directly ahead."

Fury used the car as a battering ram, slamming through stopped cars and even pushing them against the commandos trying to kill him. They had jumped out of their cars and were firing at him again, but he stayed just far enough ahead to get to the clearer part of Seventeenth Avenue. But his car was too damaged to stay clear for long, and soon two of the police cars were on either side of him again. The assassins inside fired at him, but Fury pressed back into the seat and stayed out of their field of fire.

He saw an approaching intersection and slammed on his brakes. The two police cars rocketed ahead and a moving truck passing through the intersection crashed into both of them, knocking them out of commission. "Get me off the grid!" he shouted as he swerved onto a side street.

"Calculating route to secure location," the computer said.

That was when Fury saw a masked figure, all in black, standing in the middle of the road. He watched Fury's battered SUV accelerate toward him. Aiming carefully, he fired a small disk that skipped off the road and exploded under Fury's car, flipping it upside down. The car skidded to a halt on its roof. Inside, Fury was dizzy and in terrible pain. He had blood in his eye from cuts on his face. He hurt in more places than he could count. His arm wasn't the only thing broken now.

The masked man approached, drawing a gun. Fury had one last thing he could do. He might have been badly injured, but he wasn't done quite yet. He dug in the glove compartment and came out with a compact laser torch. Good thing DC had a lot of tunnels under its streets....

By the time the figure in black got to Fury's car, he was gone. The hole he'd cut in the street still smoked around the edges.

CHAPTER 14

As he walked down the hall to his apartment, Steve ran into his neighbor Kate. She was carrying a laundry basket and talking on the phone. Everyone seemed to be on the phone all the time. "So sweet," she was saying. "That is so nice. I got to go, though. Okay. Bye." She dropped the phone in her laundry and looked at Steve with a sheepish smile. "My aunt, she's kind of an insomniac."

"Yeah," Steve said. "Hey, if you want…" Suddenly he was nervous. Maybe Natasha was right that he should ask her out, but it had been a long time since Steve asked a girl out. "If you want, you're welcome to use my machine. Might be cheaper than the one in the basement."

She raised an eyebrow. "Oh, yeah? What's it cost?"

"A cup of coffee?"

She smiled. "Thank you, but I already have a load in downstairs, and you really don't want my scrubs in your machine. I just finished a rotation in the infectious disease ward, so..."

Steve knew what she was saying. Thanks but no thanks. "Well, I'll keep my distance," he said.

"Hopefully not too far," she said. "Oh, and I think you left your stereo on."

"Oh," Steve said. He knew for a fact he hadn't left his stereo on. "Right. Thank you."

Kate went to do her laundry and Steve cautiously entered his apartment. If his stereo was on, someone had been in there. Who? Why? It didn't take long for him to find out.

Sitting in the light of a single lamp on Steve's living room couch was Nick Fury. Bloodied, exhausted, but still sharp. He waited for Steve to react to his presence. Steve was confused, but he could also tell something was wrong. "I don't remember giving you a key," he said.

"You really think I'd need one? My wife kicked me out."

"I didn't know you were married."

"A lot of things you don't know about me." He turned out the lamp and showed Steve the screen of his phone. On it he had typed EARS EVERYWHERE.

Who was listening? And after the argument they'd had earlier that day, what was Fury doing in his apartment? "I know, Nick," Steve said. "That's the problem."

"I'm sorry to have to do this, but I had no place else to crash." Fury showed Steve his phone again. S.H.I.E.L.D. COMPROMISED.

Steve played along, trying to think of a way to ask who else knew they'd been infiltrated. "Who else knows about your wife?"

"Just..." YOU AND ME. "My friends."

Did he mean that, or was he saying it just for whoever might be listening in? "Is that what we are?" Steve asked.

"That's up to you," Fury said.

Suddenly, something shattered and Fury cried out and collapsed to the floor. Steve spun and saw the bullet hole through the window. He knelt next to Fury, who was lying on his back. Steve had seen a lot of men with gunshot wounds in the war, and he could tell this one was bad.

"Don't...trust...anyone," Fury wheezed. He held up the USB drive Natasha had taken from the *Lemurian Star*. Steve took it and put it in his pocket. Then Fury's eyes closed and Steve heard banging on his front door. He got up to answer it.

"Captain Rogers?" It was Kate, from across the hall. Only she was all business and carrying a gun. "Captain, I'm Agent 13 of S.H.I.E.L.D. Special Service."

"Kate?"

"I'm assigned to protect you." She looked past Steve into his apartment.

"On whose order?"

"His." She went to Fury and quickly examined him. Then she spoke into a comm. "Foxtrot is down, he's unresponsive. I need EMTs."

"Do we have a 20 on the shooter?" The voice on the other line was asking for the shooter's location.

Steve looked out the window. He saw a gleam of metal. Someone was moving on the roof of the building across the street. "Tell him I'm in pursuit," he said, and grabbed his shield.

He charged through his apartment's front window, sailed across the street, and crashed through the window of the office building across the street. Then he ran straight through the building, punching through windows and doors to keep as straight a path as he could. Luckily most of these new buildings' interior walls were just made out of drywall. Steve ran through them like they were paper. He hit a steel-reinforced wall once and had to make a detour, but he still got to the other side of the building and out onto the roof with the shooter in view.

Steve flung his shield at the target. It was a perfect throw, head-high and right on target...but at the last moment the shooter spun and shot out an arm to catch Steve's shield in midflight!

Astonished, Steve watched the shooter hold his shield out like a Frisbee. His left arm was made of some kind of metal. Over the mask, his eyes glittered with hate.

Then he threw the shield back at Steve, who caught it, but the force of the throw drove him back several steps. By the time he regained his balance, the shooter had disappeared. When Steve reached the edge of the roof, he could see no sign of where the shooter might have gone.

CHAPTER 15

By the time Steve got back to his apartment, an ambulance had already taken Fury to the hospital, probably with Kate—Agent 13. Steve got there as fast as he could. Maria Hill was already there. Natasha got there a few minutes later and they watched the surgeons work on Fury from an observation room.

"Is he gonna make it?" Natasha asked. Steve had never seen her look emotional like this before.

"I don't know," he said.

"Tell me about the shooter."

There wasn't much to tell. Black mask, black clothing...
"He's fast. Strong. Had a metal arm."

Natasha turned to Maria Hill. "Ballistics?"

"Three slugs, no rifling. Completely untraceable."

Natasha looked at her. "Soviet made," she said.

Maria looked surprised that Natasha would assume this. "Yeah," she said.

Natasha knew something. Steve could tell that, but he couldn't exactly ask her what. Not right now. The time to investigate was later. Right now they just had to be together and hope Fury would pull through. Natasha was asking questions to distract herself from her feelings. Steve stayed out of the way.

"He's in V-tach," one of the nurses said. On Fury's monitor, the numbers representing his vital signs dropped. Fast. "Crash cart coming in."

"BP's dropping," another nurse said.

"Defibrillator!" the doctor ordered. "I want you to charge him at one hundred."

"Don't do this to me, Nick," Natasha said softly.

"Stand back," the doctor said. He tested the pads. "Three, two, one. Clear."

Fury's body jumped as the defibrillator shocked him. The doctor held the pads up. "Pulse?"

"No pulse," the nurse said.

"Okay, two hundred, please," the doctor said. "Stand back! Three, two, one. Clear!"

Another shock, and Fury's body jumped again. Then he lay still. The numbers on the monitor dropped to zero. All the lines were flat.

"Get me epinephrine!" the doctor said. That was a last resort, a powerful stimulant shot that would start the patient's heart beating again. The nurse gave Fury a large dose of it. Then she bent over with a stethoscope.

"Pulse?" the doctor asked.

She shook her head. "Negative." Even the epinephrine hadn't been able to restart Fury's heart.

The doctors and nurses all stopped working. They'd done everything they could.

"Don't do this to me, Nick. Don't do this to me." Tears formed in Natasha's eyes. Steve knew she had very few close relationships in the world, and one of them was with Nick Fury. He was practically the only person who ever got through her shell of evasion and saw the real Natasha Romanoff.

And now they had just watched Nick Fury die.

The doctors started stripping off their gloves and masks. "What's the time?" one of them asked.

"1:03, Doctor," the head nurse said.

"Time of death 1:03 a.m.," the doctor said.

They stood with Nick's body for a while after he was wheeled out of surgery. Steve stood apart from them, thinking about the USB drive in his pocket. Who could he trust to tell about it? He wasn't good with cloak-and-dagger stuff. He was a soldier. He thought about it, and thought about what Nick had said before he was shot. The shock of Nick's death had thrown Steve off. He wasn't sure what to do next.

Then Maria Hill said, "I need to take him."

Natasha laid a hand on Fury's head. Steve knew this was a terrible loss for her. Fury had saved her and given her the chance to make a new life for herself. He had been a friend, guide, mentor.

"Natasha," Steve said quietly. He had to ask her a few things, and they really couldn't wait.

She finished saying her silent good-bye and left without a word to Steve or Maria Hill.

Steve followed her out into the hall. "Natasha!"

She turned to face him. "Why was Fury in your apartment?"

"I don't know," Steve said. He could tell from the look on her face that she didn't believe him.

"Cap, they want you back at S.H.I.E.L.D.," Rumlow said. He and the rest of the S.T.R.I.K.E. team were in the hospital in case the shooter came back for another crack at Captain America.

"Yeah, give me a second," he said. Steve had to finish the conversation with Natasha. She could help in ways most other people couldn't.

"They want you now," Rumlow said.

Steve turned and said, "Okay." Meaning, *wait a minute.*

"You're a terrible liar," she said. This was true, and Steve knew it. He didn't like lying. But if Natasha could see through him, maybe that would get her started looking into whatever had happened to Fury before he'd come to Steve's apartment.

Or what if she was part of it? S.H.I.E.L.D. COMPROMISED, Fury had said. Who was compromised and who was still loyal?

Steve watched her go, completely at a loss for what to do next. Then he got himself back on track. *Think like Fury would*, Cap told himself. A moment later he had the USB drive stashed in a safe place—a rarely used vending machine—because he didn't know what would happen when he got back to the Triskelion.

CHAPTER 16

What happened was that first thing in the morning, Steve was escorted into a meeting with Alexander Pierce. He was a serious bigwig, and Steve was always nervous when he met people like Pierce. Steve was just a soldier. He saw what needed doing, and he did it. Policy decisions were for other people.

But with Nick Fury gone, Steve didn't know what was going to happen next. Agent 13 was there. She nodded at him. "Captain Rogers."

He nodded back. "Neighbor."

Pierce looked up from his desk as Steve spoke to Agent 13. "Ah. Captain. I'm Alexander Pierce."

"Sir, it's an honor." They shook hands.

"The honor's mine, Captain. My father served in the 101st. Come on in." He got Steve into his office and showed him a photo of himself and Nick Fury in front of a building that Steve would have guessed was in South America somewhere. "That photo was taken five years after Nick and I met, when I was at State Department in Bogotá," Pierce said. "ELN rebels took the embassy and security got me out, but the rebels took hostages." Pierce got the distant look in his eye of someone remembering a story as he told it. Steve didn't know much about politicians, but he did know they liked to tell stories about themselves. "Nick was deputy chief of the S.H.I.E.L.D. station there, and he comes to me with a plan. He wants to storm the building through the sewers. I said, 'No, we'll negotiate.' Turned out, the ELN didn't negotiate, so they put out a kill order. They stormed the basement, and what do they find? They find it empty." They sat together at the conference table in Pierce's office. "Nick had ignored my direct order, and carried out an unauthorized military operation on foreign soil, and saved the lives of a dozen political officers, including my daughter's."

"So you gave him a promotion."

"I've never had any cause to regret it." Pierce looked at Steve like he was making sure Steve understood the point of his story. Then he got down to business. "Captain, why was Nick in your apartment last night?"

"I don't know."

"Did you know it was bugged?"

"I did, because Nick told me."

"Did he tell you he was the one who bugged it?" Steve didn't answer. He didn't know if that was true, or why Pierce wanted to see him. "I want you to see something," he said, and started a video on a wall screen.

The screen showed Georges Batroc in a prison cell being interrogated. *So they got him*, Steve thought. *Good*. "Is that live?"

"Yeah," Pierce said. "They picked him up last night in a not-so-safe house in Algiers."

Batroc had run home. Everyone did sooner or later. "Are you saying he's a suspect?"

"Assassination isn't Batroc's line. No, it's more complicated than that." Pierce paused, deciding how to approach the explanation. "Batroc was hired anonymously to attack the *Lemurian Star*. And he was contacted by e-mail and paid by wire transfer, and then the money was run through seventeen fictitious accounts. The last one going to a holding company that was registered to a Jacob Veech."

Pierce looked at Cap, but the name didn't mean anything to him. "Am I supposed to know who that is?"

"Not likely. Veech died six years ago. His last address was 1435 Elmhurst Drive. When I first met Nick, his mother lived at 1437."

Now Steve understood what Pierce was getting at. "Are you saying Fury hired the pirates? Why?"

"The prevailing theory was that the hijacking was a cover for the acquisition and sale of classified intelligence," Pierce said. "The sale went sour and that led to Nick's death."

Steve shook his head. "If you really knew Nick Fury, you'd know that's not true."

"Why do you think we're talking?" Pierce asked. Steve relaxed a little. Pierce had been testing him. He wouldn't have been able to stay in the room with someone who could believe Nick Fury was a traitor.

"See, I took a seat on the council not because I wanted to, but because Nick asked me to, because we were both realists," Pierce explained. He walked to the window and looked out over the city. "We knew that, despite all the diplomacy and the handshaking and the rhetoric, to build a really better world sometimes means having to tear the old one down. And that makes enemies. Those people that call you dirty because you got the guts to stick your hands in the mud and try to build something better. And the idea that those people could be happy today makes me really, really angry."

Pierce took a moment to gather himself before he got too emotional. "Captain, you were the last one to see Nick alive. I don't think that's an accident. And I don't think you do, either. So, I'm going to ask again. Why was he there?"

"He told me not to trust anyone," Steve said.

"I wonder if that included him."

Steve didn't know how to answer that, so he stuck to the simple facts. "I'm sorry. Those were his last words. Excuse me." He started for the door.

"Captain, somebody murdered my friend and I'm gonna find out why. Anyone gets in my way, they're gonna regret it." Pierce looked at Steve, and for a moment Steve saw the coldhearted operative behind the facade of the handsome politician. "Anyone," Pierce repeated.

"Understood," Steve said. He felt the same way. But at the same time, he had a feeling he and Pierce weren't one hundred percent on the same page...but he couldn't see just how yet.

CHAPTER 17

Leaving Pierce's office, Steve got on the elevator to the next floor down, where he was joined by Brock Rumlow and some of the S.T.R.I.K.E. team. "Cap," Rumlow said with a nod.

Steve nodded back. "Rumlow."

"Evidence Response found some fibers on the roof they want us to see. You want me to get the tac team ready?"

Steve looked out the elevator's glass wall, over the city. He was still digesting his conversation with Pierce. He wasn't sure what to do next. In any case, forensic analysis wasn't his thing. Let the scientists and techs do their work, and then he would do his. "No, let's wait and see what it is first."

"Right." Rumlow stood facing away from Steve, in front of the doors. The rest of his team had spread out to the corners of the elevator. Steve got a warning prickle on the back of his neck. This didn't feel like a group of guys who were just standing in an elevator on their way to somewhere. One of them rested a hand on the handle of his Taser. That wasn't something an experienced soldier did with a weapon unless he was planning to use it.

The elevator stopped and more S.T.R.I.K.E. operatives got on. "I'm sorry about what happened with Fury," Rumlow said quietly to Steve. "It's messed up, what happened to him."

"Thank you," Steve said. He noted two of the S.T.R.I.K.E. team fiddling with something in their hands. The operatives were all evenly spaced around the elevator, with Steve right in the middle.

The elevator stopped again and two more S.T.R.I.K.E. men pressed their way in, including Rumlow's number two, Jack Rollins. Steve now stood in the middle of a formation of eight highly trained and probably armed S.T.R.I.K.E. team commandos. S.H.I.E.L.D. COMPROMISED, he thought. This whole thing had been staged. Rumlow had tried to set him at ease while the rest of his men got themselves arranged and ready, but they stuck to their tactical training a little too closely. It was now obvious to Steve that he'd been set up. Maybe Pierce was in on it and maybe he wasn't, but one way or another Brock Rumlow and the S.T.R.I.K.E. team had known when to make their move.

Now it was time for Steve to make his.

When you were outnumbered and you couldn't choose the battleground, what you had to do was seize the initiative. Get the enemy on their heels for a moment so you could even out the numbers a little. In this case, Steve decided the best way to do that was to turn their ambush against them. He waited until the elevator doors were closing. Then he said, "Before we get started, does anyone want to get out?"

There was a pause. Then Rollins snapped out his Taser and spun, driving it at Steve. He dodged it as someone got an arm around his throat. The Taser sparked against one of the other S.T.R.I.K.E. commandos and knocked him out. Steve used the man holding him as leverage and kicked out with both feet, planting them in Rumlow's chest. Then the whole S.T.R.I.K.E. team was all over Steve. Some of them had weapons, some didn't. One of them got a magnetic cuff around Steve's right arm, but he fought to keep it away from the metal door frame and flung it away. Then another S.T.R.I.K.E. soldier got one of the cuffs on his other arm and pinned it against the door. Rumlow wedged his Taser into the small of Steve's back. His whole body lit up, but he snapped an elbow back and knocked Rumlow away. Fighting with one arm now, Steve took some punches, but he gave out a lot more, and by the time he'd managed to yank his arm free, Rumlow was the only S.T.R.I.K.E. commando left.

He backed away from Steve, as far as the elevator car would let him, brandishing two Tasers. "Whoa, big guy. I just want you to know, Cap, this isn't personal!"

As he said the last word, he lunged at Cap, lighting him up with the Tasers again. Taking the pain, Steve hit Rumlow with a combination and then got both hands on him and threw him straight up. Rumlow smashed into the elevator's steel-reinforced glass ceiling and collapsed back down to the floor.

Right, Steve thought. *You had Fury killed; now you're trying to kill me too.*

"It kind of feels personal," he said, and picked up his shield. He broke the cuff off and opened the door.

A whole tactical response team waited outside, guns leveled. "Drop the shield and put your hands in the air!"

Steve whirled out of the way of their guns and destroyed

the elevator's control panel, sending the elevator into a free fall. It jammed several floors down, and he tried to wedge the door open. There were more soldiers on that floor, so he stopped.

"Give it up, Rogers! Get that door open! You have nowhere to go!" one of the soldiers shouted through the door.

That wasn't exactly true, Steve thought. He couldn't go out the door, but there was always the window. Good thing it was a glass elevator. He lowered his shoulder and smashed through into open space, falling the whole distance from the twenty-fifth floor to the glass ceiling over the atrium on the Triskelion's ground floor. He hit the floor hard in a shower of glass, shield first, and needed a minute to get his bearings. But there was no time to rest. He had to keep moving before Rumlow's team got down to this level.

CHAPTER 18

Sitwell couldn't believe what he was seeing. A twenty-story fall, and Cap was shaking himself off like he'd just tripped and fallen. Around him, people stared or ran away from the flying glass. "Are you kidding me?" Sitwell said. "He's headed for the garage. Lock down the bridge."

Steve got to his motorcycle and made it out of the garage just ahead of the lowering blast doors. He didn't know where he was going just yet, but if he didn't get out of the Triskelion now, he never would.

A spiked barrier deployed in front of him, and at the

same time a Quinjet flew overhead and turned around to hover over the bridge and face him. A voice blared through its external speaker. "Stand down, Captain Rogers. Stand down." Its nose turret started to spin up, ready to fire. "Repeat, stand down."

Not gonna happen, Steve thought. He accelerated. Machine gun bullets tore up the surface of the bridge around him. He wove in an evasive pattern, then threw the shield at the Quinjet. The shield curved up and then over, jamming into one of the Quinjet's rotors. That wing dipped from the loss of power, and Steve jumped from his motorcycle onto the wing. He jerked the shield free and the Quinjet slewed back level, almost throwing Steve off. He flung the shield in a bank shot and cracked both of the housings on its rear engines. Flames started to shoot out of the broken thrusters and Steve leaped clear, landing on the free side of the spiked barrier. The Quinjet spun down and crashed on its belly on the bridge.

Sitwell, Steve thought. The voice coming over the speaker had belonged to Jasper Sitwell...who had also been on the *Lemurian Star*. Steve was starting to figure a few things out. Now he needed to be able to share them with someone—and he needed that USB drive. He ran.

"Eyes here," Sitwell said in the briefing room fifteen minutes later. Every agent in the room looked at him. "Whatever your op is, bury it. This is level one. Contact DOT. All traffic lights in the district go red. Shut all runways at BWI, IAD, and Reagan. All security cameras in the city go through this monitor right here. Scan all open sources, phones, computers, PDAs. Whatever. If someone tweets about this guy, I want to know about it."

Agent 13 spoke up. "With all due respect, if S.H.I.E.L.D. is conducting a manhunt for Captain America, we deserve to know why."

Secretary Pierce broke into the conversation before Sitwell could answer. They all knew him as one of the top officials in S.H.I.E.L.D., and the organization's main contact with the regular American government. "Because he lied to us," Pierce said. "Captain Rogers has information regarding the death of Director Fury. He refused to share it. As difficult as this is to accept, Captain America is a fugitive from S.H.I.E.L.D."

CHAPTER 19

The first thing Steve did when he got out of the Triskelion was return to the hospital where Nick Fury had died. The thumb drive was there, and he needed to know what was on it. He strolled down the hallway toward the vending machine on the main floor, and looked behind the same candy bars.

It was gone.

Who—?

Then he saw Natasha's reflection over his shoulder.

He grabbed her and dragged her into a small room off the main hallway. "Where is it?" He knew she'd taken the

USB drive. There was no other reason for her to stage her appearance like that.

"Safe," she said.

He kept her pinned up against the wall. "Do better."

She didn't look scared. "Where did you get it?"

"Why would I tell you?"

"Fury gave it to you. Why?"

So she knew. He decided to turn her questions back on her. If she knew Fury had given it to Steve, she might know other things, too. "What's on it?" Steve asked.

"I don't know."

He didn't believe her. "Stop lying."

"I only act like I know everything, Rogers," she said.

"I bet you knew Fury hired the pirates, didn't you?" Steve was still trying to put that together. Why would he do that? Why send Cap and the rest of the team into harm's way?

"Well, it makes sense," she said. "The ship was dirty, Fury needed a way in, so do you."

That was the difference between him and Natasha, Steve thought. She was never surprised when people did the wrong thing...or the risky thing. Did he really know her at all? Could he trust her? As far as Steve could tell, she was playing some kind of game with him and he didn't like it. He needed to know what she knew about Fury's death, and he needed to know it now.

"I'm not gonna ask you again," he said, gripping her arms.

She paused. "I know who killed Fury," she said. "Most of the intelligence community doesn't believe he exists. The ones that do call him the Winter Soldier. He's credited with over two dozen assassinations in the last fifty years."

A fifty-year career for an assassin? That wasn't physically possible unless they were dealing with another Enhanced, or some crazy life-extension technology. Steve doubted that. "So he's a ghost story," Steve said.

"Five years ago, I was escorting a nuclear engineer out of Iran. Somebody shot out my tires near Odessa. We lost control, went straight over a cliff. I pulled us out. But the Winter Soldier was there. I was covering my engineer, so he shot him straight through me." She lifted her shirt to show the scar, just above her left hip. "Soviet slug. No rifling. Bye-bye, bikinis."

"Yeah, I bet you look terrible in them now."

She ignored that. "Going after him is a dead end. I know, I've tried." She held out the USB drive. "Like you said, he's a ghost story."

Steve wasn't ready to let go of the pursuit. He accepted the USB drive. "Well, let's find out what the ghost wants."

Alexander Pierce had a lot on his plate. S.H.I.E.L.D. was in disarray after the killing of Nick Fury, the World Security Council was unhappy with the Project Insight delay, and everyone wanted to blame him. He was in charge, so he had some blame coming. Fair enough. But he also had other plans going on that right now were making him look bad...but soon enough that would change. Before then, he would have to placate the council and make sure that his plans for S.H.I.E.L.D. were still in place.

"Nick Fury was murdered in cold blood," he said, pretending to be astonished at the council's reaction. "To any reasonable person, that would make him a martyr, not a traitor."

"You know what makes him a traitor?" Powell shot back. "Hiring a mercenary to hijack his own ship."

Councilor Singh picked up this idea. "Nick Fury used your friendship to coerce this council into delaying Project Insight. A project he knew would expose his own illegal operations. At best, he lied to you. At worst..."

"Are you calling for my resignation?" Pierce asked. It was fine with him. He had plans bigger than being in the State Department. "I've got a pen and paper right here."

"That discussion can be tabled for a later time," Hawley said.

Right, Pierce thought. So far this conversation was going exactly as he had planned. "But you do want to have a discussion?" he said, to force them to put their cards on the table...while he kept his own close to the vest.

"We've already had it, Mr. Secretary," Powell said. "This council moves to immediately reactivate Project Insight." He smiled at Pierce the way you smile at someone when you know you have them beat. "If you want to say something snappy, now would be a good time."

Pierce had nothing to say. Let the councilors think they had beaten him. Nobody out-planned Alexander Pierce.

Nobody.

CHAPTER 20

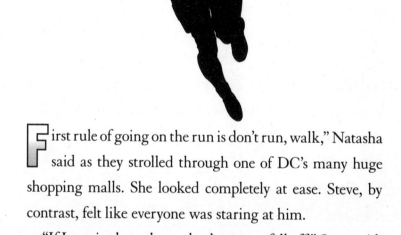

irst rule of going on the run is don't run, walk," Natasha said as they strolled through one of DC's many huge shopping malls. She looked completely at ease. Steve, by contrast, felt like everyone was staring at him.

"If I run in these shoes, they're gonna fall off," Steve said. Natasha had dressed him as some kind of hipster, with shoes that felt like their soles were made out of paper. Steve preferred boots on his feet. She had also put fake glasses on him, big plastic frames like the ones scientists wore when he was a kid. Everything eventually made a comeback.

They found a computer store and wandered in to use an

open machine at the back. It was one of the places where you could fool around on their machines as much as you wanted, in case you decided to buy one. "The drive has a level six homing program, so as soon as we boot up, S.H.I.E.L.D. will know exactly where we are," Natasha said.

Steve looked around. A mall, especially the back of a store, was not the best place to be if you were trying to avoid pursuit. "How much time will we have?"

"About nine minutes from now," she said, inserting the USB drive. "Fury was right about that ship. Somebody's trying to hide something. This drive is protected by some sort of AI. It keeps rewriting itself to counter my commands."

"Can you override it?"

"The person who developed this is slightly smarter than me," she said as she worked. "Slightly. I'm gonna try running a tracer." She spawned a new program that started probing the drive's security. "This is a program that S.H.I.E.L.D. developed to track hostile malware, so if we can't read the file, maybe we can find out where it came from." Steve nodded. At least that would give them something to go on.

A store employee came up to greet them. "Can I help you guys with anything?"

Natasha smiled at him. "Oh, no. My fiancé was just helping me with some honeymoon destinations."

Steve nodded. "Right. We're getting married."

"Congratulations. Where are you guys thinking about going?" The employee caught sight of the screen of the computer Natasha was working on. It showed a large map of New Jersey.

"New Jersey," Steve said.

It wasn't a very common honeymoon destination. "Oh," the employee said.

To distract him, Steve pointed at his face. "I have the exact same glasses."

Natasha looked over and nodded. "Wow, you two are practically twins," she said.

"Yeah, I wish." He pointed at Steve admiringly. "Specimen. If you guys need anything, I've been Aaron."

"Thank you," Natasha said. Aaron left to help other customers.

Steve was getting antsy. The clock was ticking. "You said nine minutes. Come on."

"Relax," Natasha said. "Got it."

The screen showed a magnified image of a complex in Wheaton, New Jersey. Steve got a strange feeling seeing that name after so many years.

"You know it?" Natasha asked.

"I used to. Let's go." She pulled out the USB drive and they got moving.

Right away Steve spotted the S.T.R.I.K.E. team hunting them. "Standard tac team," he said quietly. "Two behind, two across, and two coming straight at us. If they make us, I'll engage, you hit the south escalator to the metro."

"Shut up and put your arm around me," Natasha said. "Laugh at something I said."

"What?"

"Do it."

Steve did, and even though the laugh sounded completely fake to his ears, the pair of S.T.R.I.K.E. commandos walked right by without giving them a second glance.

There would be others . . . and there was Brock Rumlow. "Kiss me," Natasha said as Rumlow got closer to them. They were going down the escalator and he was coming up. No way was Rumlow going to miss them.

"What?"

"Public displays of affection make people very uncomfortable."

"Yes, they do."

She laid a memorable kiss on Steve that lasted most of the way down to the next floor. Rumlow passed by, not taking any notice of them.

"You still uncomfortable?" Natasha asked with a little gleam in her eye when they reached the bottom of the escalator.

"It's not exactly the word I would use," Steve said. Her diversion had worked. They were clear. Now all they had to do was find some transportation.

CHAPTER 21

our hours later Natasha and Steve were driving in a nice pickup truck, and when they hit the New Jersey state line, Natasha asked the question that had been on her mind since the mall. "Where did Captain America learn how to steal a car?"

"Nazi Germany."

"Mmm." She nodded.

"And we're borrowing," he said. "Take your feet off the dash."

He was such a Boy Scout, she thought. "All right, I have

a question for you, which you do not have to answer. I feel like, if you don't answer it, though, you're kind of answering it, you know?"

"What?"

"Was that your first kiss since 1945?"

He glanced over at her and then back at the road, embarrassed. "That bad, huh?"

"I didn't say that."

"Well, it kind of sounds like that's what you're saying."

"No, I didn't. I just wondered how much practice you've had."

Now she was just fooling with him. "You don't need practice," Steve said.

"Everybody needs practice."

"It was not my first kiss since 1945," he insisted. "I'm ninety-five, I'm not dead."

"Nobody special, though?"

Here we go again, Steve thought. He chuckled. "Believe it or not, it's kind of hard to find someone with shared life experience."

"Well, that's all right. You just make something up."

"What, like you?" He wished it was that easy.

"I don't know," she said. "The truth is a matter of

circumstance. It's not all things to all people, all the time. Neither am I."

All of a sudden the conversation had taken a serious turn. "That's a tough way to live," Steve said. He wondered what she'd been through to put such a cynical spin on the way she saw the world.

She had a distant expression on her face as she answered him. "It's a good way not to die, though."

Steve still sympathized, but he also needed to know who he could count on, and Natasha's evasions made him nervous. "You know, it's kind of hard to trust someone when you don't know who that someone really is," he said.

"Yeah." She looked at him and asked, "Who do you want me to be?"

What kind of a question was that? How could a person choose who they were? Steve sure couldn't. But maybe that was what made him different from Natasha. "How about a friend?" he said, trying to keep it simple.

She didn't laugh, but he could tell she wanted to. "Well, there's a chance you might be in the wrong business, Rogers."

Steve thought she might be right...but there wasn't much he could do about it now.

A little while later they turned down a winding side road and parked at a gate next to a guardhouse with peeling paint and a visible hole in the roof. "This is it?" Steve asked.

Natasha checked her GPS and said, "The file came from these coordinates."

"So did I," Steve said. "This camp is where I was trained."

"Change much?"

"A little." He remembered training here. The drill sergeants shouting... *Let's go! Let's go! Double time! Come on, Rogers, move it!* ... all the marching, all the combat drills... all before he had gone to the war and never come home.

Natasha was observing the camp. "This is a dead end. Zero heat signatures, zero waves, not even radio. Whoever wrote the file must have used a router to throw people off." She saw Steve looking at an ordnance storage building, as they got out of the car. "What is it?"

"Army regulations forbid storing munitions within five hundred yards of the barracks. This building is in the wrong place." He broke the lock with his shield and they went inside.

At the bottom of a staircase Steve found a light switch in the dark and tried it. Surprisingly, the lights came on.

"This is S.H.I.E.L.D. Maybe where it started." Steve had been in bases like this one. The early Stark-style bases, the ones that had been put together under the name S.H.I.E.L.D. He had pretty much been created in one. They looked like regular military on the surface, but there was always something else going on when you looked a little deeper. "And there's Stark's father," Natasha said, pointing at a large oil portrait.

"Howard," Steve said. He'd met him a few times.

Natasha was looking at the picture next to the Howard Stark portrait. "Who's the girl?"

It was Peggy Carter. Steve remembered her looking like that. Serious, businesslike. She knew how important her job was even before the founding of S.H.I.E.L.D. Every time he saw a picture of her, it hit him all over again how much he'd missed. He didn't say anything. This wasn't the time to bare his soul to Natasha.

They kept looking because there was something the file was leading them to and they hadn't found it yet. Steve noticed something odd about a row of floor-to-ceiling steel shelves. "If you're already working in a secret office..." He pulled the shelves along the wall with a squeak of rust. "Why do you need to hide the elevator?"

CHAPTER 22

The elevator was much more recent than the rest of the facility. It had a digital keypad that Natasha cracked in seconds, and then they were riding it down. It opened into a large room, dimly lit. But as they walked into it, lights came on all around them. The room was full of old computers. Real old. Like the kind of technology Steve could almost recognize from before he'd gone into the ice. Howard Stark would have laughed at this stuff, and Tony Stark would have called an antique dealer to haul it away. "This can't be the data point," Natasha said. "This technology is ancient."

But oddly, there was a small dock for USB ports sitting on a dusty table in front of a bank of buttons and switches. Someone had been here recently. Natasha plugged the thumb drive into it. All around them, the old machines whirred to life and a prompt appeared on one of the monitors: INITIALIZE SYSTEM?

"Y-E-S spells yes." Natasha entered the word. "Shall we play a game?" She glanced at Steve. "It's from a movie that was really..."

"I know," Steve said. "I saw it." *War Games.* He'd thought it was kind of goofy, but that was because he didn't trust computers.

A camera swiveled to look at each of them in turn, and flickering green lines resolved into the image of a face on the largest monitor. "Rogers, Steven, born 1918. Romanoff, Natalia Alianovna, born 1984."

Steve got a chill as he recognized the voice.

"It's some kind of recording," Natasha said.

"I am not a recording, Fräulein. I may not be the man I was when the captain took me prisoner in 1945. But I am." Another monitor lit up with a mug shot that Steve remembered from the war.

Natasha looked at Steve. "You know this thing?"

Steve nodded. "Arnim Zola was a German scientist who worked for the Red Skull. He's been dead for years."

"First correction: I am Swiss," Zola said. "Second: Look around you. I have never been more alive. In 1972, I received a terminal diagnosis. Science could not save my body. My mind, however, that was worth saving, on two hundred thousand feet of data banks. You are standing in my brain."

"How did you get here?" Steve asked.

"Invited," Zola said.

"It was Operation Paperclip after World War II," Natasha said. "S.H.I.E.L.D. recruited German scientists with strategic value."

"They thought I could help their cause," Zola added. "I also helped my own."

Steve didn't believe it. "Hydra died with the Red Skull."

"Cut off one head, two more shall take its place." Zola sounded smug.

"Prove it."

"Accessing archive." Zola paused. Another monitor lit up and started showing images. "Hydra was founded on the belief that humanity could not be trusted with its own freedom. What we did not realize was that if you try to take that freedom, they resist. The war taught us much. Humanity needed to surrender its freedom willingly." Zola spoke over a montage of film footage from World War II—and then the years after. Steve saw himself in some of it, back in the war. Before the seventy years he'd lost. He also saw the Red Skull and Howard Stark...."After the war, S.H.I.E.L.D. was founded, and I was recruited. The new Hydra grew, a beautiful parasite inside S.H.I.E.L.D. For seventy years, Hydra has been secretly feeding crisis, reaping war, and when history did not cooperate, history was changed."

"That's impossible," Natasha said. "S.H.I.E.L.D. would have stopped you."

"Accidents will happen. Hydra created a world so chaotic that humanity is finally ready to sacrifice its freedom to gain its security. Once a purification process is complete, Hydra's new world order will arise." Now the monitor displayed high-resolution images of the Project Insight Helicarriers. S.H.I.E.L.D. COMPROMISED, Steve thought. He hadn't figured it would be compromised by Hydra. Maybe nobody had.

"We won, Captain," Zola said. "Your death amounts to the same as your life. A zero sum."

Steve punched a hole in the monitor screen. It didn't do any good.

"As I was saying…" Zola went on from another speaker and monitor.

"What's on this drive?" Natasha interrupted.

"Project Insight requires insight. So, I wrote an algorithm."

"What kind of algorithm? What does it do?"

"The answer to your question is fascinating. Unfortunately, you shall be too dead to hear it."

As Zola spoke, the heavy doors over the elevator shaft began to close. Steve threw his shield to try to jam the doors open, but it bounced off them and skipped back to him. Natasha's phone chirped.

"Steve, we got a bogey," she said, reading the warning. "Short-range ballistic. Thirty seconds tops."

"Who fired it?"

She looked scared for the first time Steve could remember. "S.H.I.E.L.D."

"I am afraid I have been stalling, Captain," Zola said. Natasha grabbed the USB drive and Steve looked around for any kind of protection. He saw a ventilation grate in the floor and wrenched it loose. "Admit it," Zola finished. "It's better this way. We are, both of us, out of time."

With his last words, Steve and Natasha dove into the space under the ventilation grate.

The missiles hit with a sound that left both Steve and Natasha temporarily deaf. Most of the bunker collapsed immediately. Steve held up his shield, absorbing the impact of falling debris and the heat of the missile's explosion in the upper levels of the base. They held on, and when the wreckage finished collapsing on them, Steve forced his way up into the lab. There were fires all around them. Arnim Zola was gone. He'd only existed in the hard drives of these outdated computers, and now they were all blasted to fragments.

Natasha was out cold. He picked her up and carried her up to the surface. Then he saw spotlights from incoming Quinjets, and he started to move faster, carrying Natasha over the wreckage. Racing against time.

Hydra's invasion had gone further than he ever would have thought. Steve and Natasha needed to find someone they could trust.

CHAPTER 23

B rock Rumlow and his team of S.T.R.I.K.E. operatives landed in Quinjets and spread out to pick through the wreckage. It was their job to make sure Steve and Romanoff hadn't gotten out of the old base. The Zola loose end was tied up, Rumlow could tell that. But as he looked around in the debris, he could tell something else, too.

Right there, near the edge of the debris field, he saw a footprint, clear in the dust: It had been made after the explosion. Steve was alive. "Call in the asset," Rumlow said.

Alexander Pierce was going to his kitchen for a late-night snack when he saw someone standing in the shadows. He recognized the visitor. He wasn't happy to see him, exactly, but his work did have a tendency to follow him home sometimes. "I'm going to go, Mr. Pierce," his housekeeper Renata called from the living room. "You need anything before I leave?"

"No...uh, it's fine, Renata, you can go home," he said. He wanted her gone because he needed to have a delicate conversation without her around.

"Okay. Night-night," she said.

Pierce nodded. "Good night."

With his housekeeper gone, Pierce could devote his full attention to matters at hand. Namely, the Winter Soldier standing in his kitchen. "Want some milk?" he asked, to be polite. He knew the answer would be no. Pierce always offered pleasantries. But after he poured himself a glass, he got down to business. "The timetable has moved," he said. "Our window is limited. Two targets, level six. They already cost me Zola. I want confirmed death in ten hours."

The Winter Soldier's gaze lifted. He was looking at something over Pierce's shoulder.

It was Renata. "Sorry, Mr. Pierce, I...I forgot my phone," she said. She looked at the Winter Soldier and he could see the fear on her face.

Why, Pierce wondered, did people have to show up at inopportune times? Small mistakes sometimes had large consequences. "Oh, Renata," he said. "I wish you would have knocked."

CHAPTER 24

Sam Wilson had just gotten back from his morning run when there was a knock at the sliding glass door in his backyard. That was weird. The yard was fenced. Who would go back there and knock?

He pulled the blinds aside and saw Steve Rogers and Natasha Romanoff. Well, this was not going to be an ordinary morning. He slid the door open. "Hey, man," he said.

"I'm sorry about this," Steve said. "We need a place to lay low."

"Everyone we know is trying to kill us," Romanoff said.

She sounded like it wasn't the first time this had happened to her.

Sam sighed. "Not everyone," he said, and stood aside so they could come in. Then he looked around to make sure nobody was watching. It looked like the coast was clear.

Steve and Natasha got cleaned up in Sam's guest room. "You okay?" he asked her. Something seemed off with her.

"Yeah," she said, but he didn't believe it.

He sat next to her on the couch. "What's going on?"

"When I first joined S.H.I.E.L.D., I thought I was going straight," she said. "But I guess I just traded in the KGB for Hydra. I thought I knew whose lies I was telling, but I guess I can't tell the difference anymore."

That was a big confession for her, Steve thought. She never let any part of her real self show. Maybe Fury's death had broken something loose inside her. "There's a chance you might be in the wrong business," he said, trying to lighten the mood a little.

She smiled. It wasn't much of a smile, but it was something. "I owe you," she said.

"It's okay."

"If it was the other way around, and it was down to me to save your life—now you be honest with me—would you trust me to do it?"

Steve knew what she needed. Her whole life seemed like a series of lies and betrayals to her. She didn't just need someone to trust. She needed someone to trust her. "I would now," Steve said. He meant it. "And I'm always honest."

This seemed to help her. "Well, you seem pretty chipper for someone who just found out they died for nothing," she said, thinking of what Arnim Zola had said.

"Well, guess I just like to know who I'm fighting." Now that he knew the enemy was Hydra, Steve felt better. He had a clear purpose again.

Sam popped into the room. "I made breakfast," he said. "If you guys eat that sort of thing."

They did. And they were hungry. They sat down and put a dent in Sam's groceries, and then continued figuring out their situation.

"So, the question is, who at S.H.I.E.L.D. could launch a domestic missile strike?" Natasha asked them. That was where they needed to start because the answer to that question would tell them who was in charge...meaning who was the leader of the Hydra spies who had infiltrated the Triskelion.

"Pierce," Steve said.

Natasha nodded. "Who happens to be sitting on top of the most secure building in the world."

"But he's not working alone," Steve said. "Zola's algorithm was on the *Lemurian Star.*"

"So was Jasper Sitwell," Natasha said. Steve looked at her and saw that she had just figured something out. A moment later he figured it out, too: Sitwell was in on it and had been from the beginning. Steve had suspected this when he'd heard Sitwell issuing orders through the Quinjet's speakers, but at that point it was still possible Sitwell was just following someone else's orders. But if he had been part of the corruption inside S.H.I.E.L.D. for longer than that...

"So," Steve said. "The real question is, how do the two most wanted people in Washington kidnap a S.H.I.E.L.D. officer in broad daylight?"

Sam came back into the room. "The answer is, you don't." He dropped a folder on the coffee table between Steve and Natasha. Printed on the cover in large black letters was EXO-7 FALCON.

"What's this?" Steve asked.

"Call it a résumé."

Natasha looked at the file. The cover photo was of Sam in a nonstandard combat uniform, with a friend, against a desert background. Natasha recognized the desert right away. "Is this Bakhmala? The Khalid Khandil mission—that was you?" Sam nodded, and Natasha turned to Steve. "You didn't say he was a pararescue."

Steve pointed to the other man in the photo. "Is this Riley?"

"Yeah," Sam said quietly.

"I heard they couldn't bring in the choppers because of the RPGs," Natasha said. She sounded familiar with the operation Sam had been on, but Steve had never heard of it. "What did you use? A stealth chute?"

"No. These." Sam handed Steve another folder and waited for him to look at the images inside.

There sure was more to Sam Wilson than he'd thought at first. "I thought you said you were a pilot," Steve said.

"I never said pilot."

Steve shook his head. "I can't ask you to do this, Sam. You got out for a good reason."

"Dude, Captain America needs my help. There's no better reason to get back in."

Okay, Steve thought. If they had to take on Hydra and S.H.I.E.L.D., they would need all the help they could get. "Where can we get our hands on one of these things?"

"The last one is at Fort Meade," Sam said. "Behind three guarded gates and a twelve-inch steel wall."

Steve looked at Natasha. She shrugged. "Shouldn't be a problem," Steve said.

CHAPTER 25

Listen," Senator Stern said as he and Jasper Sitwell exited the private meeting room near the Capitol Building. Sitwell had just briefed him on recent developments at S.H.I.E.L.D. "I got to fly home tonight because I got some constituency problem."

"Any constituent in particular, Mr. Senator?" Sitwell asked with a grin.

"Oh, no, not really. This isn't the place to talk about it." Stern fingered Sitwell's lapel and the small gold Hydra pin on it. "This is a nice pin."

Sitwell smiled proudly. "Thank you."

Stern brought him in for a hug. "Hail Hydra," he whispered into Sitwell's ear. Then he went off with his entourage to take care of business.

Sitwell got a call and saw ALEXANDER PIERCE on the caller ID. "I need a minute," he told his S.H.I.E.L.D. team. They weren't in on the real state of affairs. "Bring the car around." As they left, he answered the phone. "Yes, sir?"

"Agent Sitwell, how was lunch? I hear the crab cakes here are delicious."

The voice did not belong to Alexander Pierce. "Who is this?"

"The good-looking guy in the sunglasses—your ten o'clock." Sitwell looked to his right. "Your other ten o'clock." Sitwell turned the other direction. "There you go." Sitwell saw him: A solid-looking African American man in jeans and a leather jacket, raising his glass of tea in a mock toast from the coffeehouse patio across the street.

"What do you want?" Sitwell asked.

"You're gonna go around the corner to your right. There's a gray car two spaces down. You and I are gonna take a ride."

Sitwell smirked. He'd been threatened before. He had no intention of doing whatever this stranger wanted him to do. "And why would I do that?"

"Because that tie looks really expensive, and I'd hate to mess it up."

Sitwell looked down and saw the bright red dot of a laser sight on his tie, about six inches below the knot. Right over his heart.

The gray car took him to another building, and before Sitwell knew what was happening, he'd been dragged up to a rooftop and Steve Rogers was shoving him across it toward the edge. "Tell me about Zola's algorithm," Steve said. Natasha Romanoff was right behind him.

"Never heard of it," Sitwell said.

"What were you doing on the *Lemurian Star*?"

"I was throwing up. I get seasick." Sitwell bumped into the knee-high parapet running around the roof and stumbled. Steve caught him but didn't let him get away from the edge.

Sitwell started to get his composure back. "Is this little display meant to insinuate that you're gonna throw me off the roof?" he asked with a smirk. "Because it's really not your style, Rogers."

Steve nodded. "You're right. It's not." He nodded at Romanoff. "It's hers."

And then Steve stepped aside and Romanoff kicked Sitwell square in the chest, knocking him off the top of the thirty-story building.

His scream faded into the distance. "Oh, wait," Natasha said. "What about that girl from Accounting, Laura..."

"Lillian," Steve corrected her. "Lip piercing, right?"

Natasha nodded. "Yeah, she's cute."

"Yeah. I'm not ready for that," Steve said.

A moment later they could hear Jasper Sitwell screaming again, and a moment after that he came flying up over the edge of the roof, in the firm grasp of Sam Wilson.

Sam wasn't wearing a costume, just his regular clothes. He wore polarized goggles against the glare and the wind...and from his shoulders sprouted twenty-foot wings jointed into a jetpack barely larger than a high school kid's backpack. This was the Exo-7 Falcon technology, and Sam was the Falcon.

He dropped Sitwell onto the roof and swung around to land. The wings folded themselves into the jetpack, which powered down. Steve and Natasha walked up to Sitwell, who wasn't smirking anymore.

"Zola's algorithm is a program for choosing Insight's targets," Sitwell panted.

"What targets?" Steve asked.

Sitwell pointed at him. "You! A TV anchor in Cairo, the undersecretary of defense, a high school valedictorian in Iowa City, Bruce Banner, Stephen Strange, anyone who's a threat to Hydra. Now, or in the future."

Steve thought that anyone who went after Banner would get more than they bargained for. But he had more questions. "In the future? How could it know?"

Sitwell chuckled. Maybe he was still scared, but he got himself together and stood to face Steve. "How could it not? The twenty-first century is a digital book. Zola taught Hydra how to read it. Your bank records, medical histories, voting patterns, e-mails, phone calls! Zola's algorithm evaluates people's past to predict their future."

"And what then?"

"Oh, my God. Pierce is gonna kill me." Sitwell clammed up.

Steve took a step forward. He wasn't going to let Sitwell stop now. "What then?" he repeated, louder this time.

"Then the Insight Helicarriers scratch people off the list," Sitwell said. "A few million at a time."

CHAPTER 26

They took Sitwell and headed for the Triskelion. "Hydra doesn't like leaks," Sitwell said from the backseat. He was worried about what was going to happen to him if Steve, Natasha, and Sam decided they didn't need him anymore.

"Then why don't you try sticking a cork in it?" Sam said. He was driving.

From the backseat next to Sitwell, Natasha said, "Insight's launching in sixteen hours. We're cutting it a little bit close here."

"I know," Steve said. "We'll use him to bypass the DNA scans and access the Helicarriers directly."

"What?" Sitwell shouted. "Are you crazy? That is a terrible, terrible idea."

He started to say something else, but just then there was a heavy bang on top of the car and a window shattered. A metallic arm reached in, yanked Sitwell out, and flung him away, onto the road. A moment later bullets started punching through the roof. Someone was up there, and Steve thought he knew who it was.

Sam slammed on the brakes and a black-clad figure tumbled out onto the road. The figure slowed himself down by dragging his metal hand on the roadway and got his balance. Then he stood to face them in the car. Traffic flowed around them in the right and left lanes, but the figure didn't look afraid.

The Winter Soldier, Steve thought. *There he is.*

A Humvee rear-ended the car hard and pushed it toward the Winter Soldier, who jumped up onto the roof of the car. He punched through the windshield and tore the steering wheel off its column. Sam shouted, and his car veered off toward the side of the highway. Natasha fired her pistol through the roof at the Winter Soldier, who jumped back onto the Humvee.

Sam's car swerved out of control. There wasn't much he could do about it. In another moment it was going to flip over.

"Hang on!" Steve said. He shoved his shield against the passenger door and broke it off its hinges. As Sam's car tipped up on two wheels, Steve, Natasha, and Sam all dove out onto the loose door, riding it like a sparking, squealing sled down the highway. Sam fell off before they stopped and rolled down the road. Ahead of them, the car flipped five or six times, pieces of it breaking off and bouncing on the pavement. They were on an overpass spanning a main avenue.

The Humvee squealed to a halt and one of the Hydra commandos inside handed the Winter Soldier a grenade launcher. He fired it at Steve. The explosion blew Steve off the overpass and through the window of a bus below. The driver swerved and crashed. Steve bounced around inside the bus. Where was his shield?

Up on the overpass, Natasha and Sam ducked behind a crashed car. Hydra commandos peppered it with machine gun fire. They split up and ran in opposite directions. The Winter Soldier fired a grenade at Natasha. She dove off the overpass just ahead of the explosion, shooting a grappling hook into the underside of the bridge and swinging herself upright onto the street below. She landed running. Then, just as she was about to come out on the other side of the bridge, she stopped.

She could see the Winter Soldier's shadow cast by the bright midday sun.

She paused, just for a moment. Then she jumped out from under the bridge and before he could draw a bead on her, she fired.

The bullet hit him squarely in the upper part of his mask, knocking him down. Then she ran again, hoping to find Steve and Sam.

Up on the bridge, the Winter Soldier shook his head. The impact knocked him off his feet. He took off his goggles. One of the lenses was cracked from Natasha's bullet. Furious, he threw the goggles away. Then he stood again and blasted away at her with his machine gun. She stayed behind cover, firing back at him until her pistols were empty. Then she kept running away down the street.

"I have her," the Winter Soldier said in Russian to the commandos. "Find him." He meant Captain America.

He jumped off the bridge and landed on an abandoned car. In no particular hurry, he started walking after Natasha. She couldn't run forever. Behind him, the Hydra commandos hung grappling hooks from a crashed car and rappelled down to the street below.

The bus had tipped over on its side. Steve was getting to his feet when the Hydra commandos started shooting into it. One of them had a heavy machine gun with six rotating barrels. The bullets tore the bus apart. Steve barely got out and found his shield on the street. They saw him and he ducked behind his shield, feeling bullets ricochet off it in every direction.

It was a tough spot to be in. He wouldn't be able to deflect every bullet if the Hydra commandos spread out and shot from different angles.

Then Sam came to the rescue. Up on the bridge, he knocked out one of the commandos and took his weapon. Firing in short bursts, he hit two of the three commandos who were aiming at Steve. Then Steve charged the commando with the heavy gun and got close enough to wrestle him down and render him unconscious.

"Go! I got this!" Sam called from the bridge. Steve had to go after the Winter Soldier before he caught up to Natasha.

CHAPTER 27

Down the street, the Winter Soldier blew up a police car with his grenade launcher. He kept walking among abandoned cars, knowing Natasha was somewhere nearby. He paused, and as the street emptied out because everyone had run away, he heard her voice. "Taking fire above and below expressway. Civilians threatened. Repeat, civilians threatened."

It was coming from the other side of a minivan in the middle of the street. Quietly the Winter Soldier armed a small spherical grenade and rolled it under the car. "I make an LZ, twenty-three hundred block of Virginia Avenue," Natasha was saying. "Rendezvous, two minutes."

The grenade clinked up against the curb—right next to where Natasha had left a phone, open and transmitting her voice. A perfect diversion.

The grenade went off, destroying the phone and a nearby car. Right then Natasha leaped out of her hiding place, on the other side of the street, and landed on the Winter Soldier's back. She tried to get a chokehold on him, but he flung her away. He was too strong. He picked up his gun and Natasha threw a tiny disk from a compartment on her belt. The disk was designed to short out electronic systems, and it worked perfectly. When it hit the Winter Soldier's metal arm, there was a popping noise and his arm went limp. He couldn't raise his machine gun.

Natasha ran, keeping several cars between herself and the Winter Soldier. Behind her, he pried the disk loose from his arm and it sparked back to life.

"Get out of the way!" she shouted as she ran around the corner. "Stay out of the way!" Civilians scattered and ran. She made another turn, and out of nowhere a bullet struck her in the shoulder, knocking her down. She hit the ground hard and tried to get up, but she was badly wounded. Shock kept her from recovering. Just ahead she saw the Winter Soldier aiming his gun at her.

Then Steve Rogers appeared, taking the Winter Soldier's gunfire on his shield and charging him. The Winter Soldier slammed a punch into the shield, hard enough to stop Steve in his tracks. He threw Steve to the street, then pulled a submachine gun from his back and started firing. Steve dodged in close and kicked the gun away. The Winter Soldier had yet another gun, a pistol. By the time he had it pointed at Steve, Steve was again too close. He knocked it out of the Winter Soldier's hand and tried to hit him with his shield. But the Winter Soldier grabbed on to the shield. They wrestled, and once the Winter Soldier got the shield away from Steve, he threw it at him. Steve dodged and the shield stuck in the back door of a van.

Now the Winter Soldier had a knife. Steve closed in on him one more time and fought him, avoiding the knife and landing powerful punches. As long as Steve avoided the blows from the cybernetic arm, he held his own. That arm was powerful enough that when the Winter Soldier missed Steve with a punch, his fist smashed a hole in the street. As they grappled, Steve found a moment to retrieve his shield. He slammed its edge into the Winter Soldier's cybernetic arm, right behind the red star on its shoulder. Then, as he flipped the Winter Soldier, he tore his mask away.

They faced each other in the street, and Steve realized with a shock that he recognized the man behind the mask.

It couldn't be. It was impossible. But he was looking at his old friend Bucky Barnes...who had fallen into an icy gorge during one of the Howling Commandos' last fights during World War II. Seventy years ago.

"Bucky?" Steve said.

CHAPTER 28

The name didn't appear to mean anything to the Winter Soldier. "Who is Bucky?"

He raised his gun. Steve was too shocked to do anything but stare.

Before the Winter Soldier could fire, the Falcon swooped in behind him and landed a two-footed kick to the back of his neck. The Winter Soldier went sprawling. When he got up to fire again, Steve was still standing in shock.

Natasha came to the rescue. She had found the Winter Soldier's grenade launcher, and though she could barely use her left arm, she fired it at him. The explosion obscured him in a fireball and a column of smoke. When the smoke cleared, he was gone.

Police cars came screaming up the street, lights and sirens blaring. No. Not police cars. S.H.I.E.L.D. cars. A response team led by Brock Rumlow charged out of the cars and surrounded Steve, Sam, and Natasha with their guns drawn.

"Drop the shield, Cap!" Rumlow shouted. "Get on your knees! Down! Don't move!"

One of the other S.H.I.E.L.D. agents looked like he was about to shoot Steve right there in the street. Steve recognized him from the fight in the elevator. All of a sudden it seemed like everyone in S.H.I.E.L.D. was actually working for Hydra.

"Put the gun down," Rumlow said. He looked up into the sky, where a news helicopter hovered, pointing cameras at the scene. "Not here."

Right, Steve thought. They didn't want to kill him where people could see.

Sam and Natasha were being arrested, too. They were in the hands of their enemies.

But all Steve could think about was seeing the face of Bucky Barnes.

"It was him," he said to Sam and Natasha in the back of

the van taking them to the Triskelion. They were all manacled. "He looked right at me like he didn't even know me."

"How is that even possible?" Sam asked. "It was, like, seventy years ago."

Steve thought he knew. "Zola. Bucky's whole unit was captured in '43. Zola experimented on him. Whatever he did helped Bucky survive the fall. They must have found him and..."

"None of that's your fault, Steve," Natasha said.

"Even when I had nothing, I had Bucky," Steve said. He couldn't believe Bucky was alive, and even more than that, he couldn't believe Bucky had tried to kill him. What had Zola done to him?

Natasha's eyes started to close. She was pale and the whole left side of her jumpsuit was wet with blood. "We need to get a doctor here," Sam said to one of the guards with them in the back of the van. "If we don't put pressure on that wound, she's gonna bleed out here in the truck."

The guard brandished a Taser. Sam leaned away from it—and then the guard drove the Taser into the other guard's chest! The second guard fell forward without a sound. The first guard pulled off her helmet...revealing the face of Maria Hill!

"Ah," she said. "That thing was squeezing my brain." She looked at Sam and then at Steve. "Who is this guy?"

Steve explained while they figured out a plan to escape. And when Brock Rumlow pulled the caravan of S.H.I.E.L.D. vehicles into a tunnel, he found the back of the van empty.

CHAPTER 29

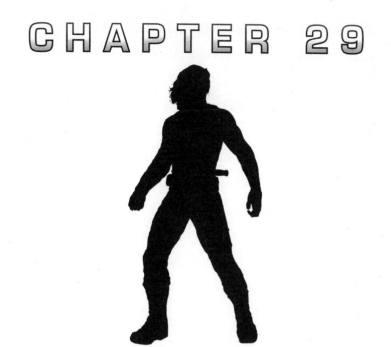

Maria Hill got Steve, Sam, and Natasha out of the commandeered van and into a vehicle of their own. She drove them to a remote S.H.I.E.L.D. facility that the Hydra infiltrators had not yet found. "GSW," she called out to the doctor who ran to meet them, using the shorthand for *gunshot wound*. "She's lost at least a pint. Maybe two."

"Let me take her," the doctor said. Natasha could barely stay on her feet. She leaned against Sam.

"She'll want to see him first," Hill said.

See who? Steve wondered. Then the doctor pulled aside a curtain and Steve felt a little flash of optimism. Maybe things would work out after all. Because behind that curtain, battered and bruised in a hospital bed but very much alive, was Nick Fury.

"About time," Fury said.

While the doctor treated Natasha, Fury started to get them up to speed. He listed off the injuries he'd suffered in the Hydra assassination attempt. "Lacerated spinal column, cracked sternum, shattered collarbone, perforated liver, and one heck of a headache."

"Don't forget your collapsed lung," the doctor said.

"Let's not forget that," Fury agreed. "Otherwise, I'm good."

Natasha couldn't believe it. "They cut you open. Your heart stopped."

"Tetrodotoxin B. Slows the pulse to one beat a minute. Banner developed it for stress. Didn't work so great for him, but we found a use for it."

"Why all the secrecy?" Steve asked. "Why not just tell us?"

"Any attempt on the director's life had to look successful," Hill said.

Fury nodded. "Can't kill you if you're already dead. Besides, I wasn't sure who to trust."

In a secret sub-basement of a downtown Washington, DC, building, Hydra technicians worked to repair the Winter Soldier's arm. He sat staring off into space, fighting against the flood of memories that threatened to drive him crazy. Steve Rogers had looked at him and said, "Bucky."

Who was Bucky? Then the Winter Soldier started to remember.

He remembered Arnim Zola, the Hydra scientist, leaning over him when he was in the hospital after falling from the train. He remembered Steve Rogers—Captain America— calling out as he fell. He remembered the snow, and being cold. He remembered feeling like he was going to die.

Then he remembered waking up in the Hydra research lab and looking at his new left arm, shining metal. *"The procedure has already started,"* Zola had said. *"You are to be the new fist of Hydra."*

Then Zola had turned to another Hydra scientist and said, *"Put him on ice."*

Bucky jerked in his chair and flung the Hydra technician across the room. The guards all turned their guns on him. He froze. He was not Bucky. There was no Bucky.

He was the Winter Soldier.

Wasn't he?

From the hall outside he heard someone say, "Sir, he's unstable. Erratic."

Then Alexander Pierce walked in and gestured for everyone to lower their guns. The Winter Soldier knew Pierce. Pierce was his mission chief. He gave the orders. Bucky—no, the Winter Soldier—waited to hear what he would say now.

"Mission report," Pierce said.

The Winter Soldier stared. "Mission report now," Pierce said. When the Winter Soldier didn't respond, Pierce slapped him in the face.

"The man on the bridge," the Winter Soldier said. "Who was he?"

"You met him earlier this week on another assignment," Pierce said.

The Winter Soldier knew that. He remembered that assignment, to extract Jasper Sitwell. But he also remembered... "I knew him," he said.

"Your work has been a gift to mankind," Pierce said. His voice was quiet and persuasive. "You shaped the century. And I need you to do it one more time. Society's at a tipping point between order and chaos. And tomorrow morning, we're gonna give it a push. But if you don't do your part, I can't do mine. And Hydra can't give the world the freedom it deserves."

"But I knew him," the Winter Soldier said.

Pierce sighed. He stood up and turned to the nearby doctor. "Prep him."

"He's been out of cryo freeze too long," the doctor objected.

"Then wipe him and start over," Pierce said.

The doctors got to work. Pierce and Rumlow left to attend to other business. Tomorrow, Project Insight would usher in a new world.

CHAPTER 30

In the S.H.I.E.L.D. bunker with Steve, Natasha, and Sam, Nick Fury held a picture of Alexander Pierce. "This man declined the Nobel Peace Prize," he said thoughtfully. "He said peace wasn't an achievement, it was a responsibility. See, it's stuff like this that gives me trust issues."

"We have to stop the launch," Natasha said. They knew enough from Sitwell to understand that tomorrow would be a very bad day for humanity if they didn't do something.

"I don't think the council's accepting my calls anymore," Fury said dryly.

Maria Hill opened a small rectangular case containing

three computer chips. They looked like memory cards, only bigger.

"What's that?" Sam asked.

She turned a laptop screen so they could all see it. On its screen was a map of the eastern United States. Washington, DC, was at the center, with a red circle around it. Lines radiated from DC out to satellite positions over Maine, Michigan, Georgia, Texas, and the Bahamas. "Once the Helicarriers reach three thousand feet, they'll triangulate with Insight satellites, becoming fully weaponized."

"We need to breach those carriers and replace their targeting blades with our own," Fury said. That's what the chips were.

"One or two won't cut it," Hill added. "We need to link all three carriers for this to work, because if even one of those ships remains operational, a whole lot of people are gonna die."

"We have to assume everyone aboard those carriers is Hydra," Fury said. "We have to get past them, insert these server blades. And maybe, just maybe, we can salvage what's left…"

Steve interrupted him. "We're not salvaging anything. We're not just taking down the carriers, Nick. We're taking down S.H.I.E.L.D."

"S.H.I.E.L.D. had nothing to do with this," Fury said.

"You gave me this mission," Steve said. "This is how it ends. S.H.I.E.L.D.'s been compromised. You said so yourself. Hydra grew right under your nose and nobody noticed."

"Why do you think we're meeting in this cave? I noticed."

That wasn't enough for Steve. He didn't think Fury understood. "How many paid the price before you did?"

"Look, I didn't know about Barnes," Fury said.

"Even if you had, would you have told me? Or would you have compartmentalized that, too? S.H.I.E.L.D., Hydra . . . it all goes."

"He's right," Maria Hill said. Fury looked from her to Natasha, who said nothing. Then he turned to Sam.

"Don't look at me," Sam said. "I do what he does, just slower."

Fury paused. Steve could see him assessing the situation and understanding that maybe things had gone further than he had understood. "Well," he said after a minute. "It looks like you're giving the orders now, Captain."

Later, Steve stood on top of the dam hiding the S.H.I.E.L.D. bunker and remembered one of the last times he'd seen

Bucky before the war. It had been right after Steve's mother died. They were walking together back to the Rogers's apartment in Brooklyn. Steve's apartment. Now he would be alone there. "We looked for you, after," Bucky had said, meaning the funeral. "My folks wanted to give you a ride to the cemetery."

"I know, I'm sorry," Steve said. "I just kind of wanted to be alone."

"How was it?" Bucky hadn't been to the burial.

"It was okay. She's next to Dad."

Bucky shifted his weight. He looked a little uncomfortable. "I was gonna ask..."

"I know what you're gonna say, Buck." The Barnes family would offer Steve a place to stay so he didn't have to be alone.

"I just..." Bucky tried to smile. "We can put the couch cushions on the floor like when we were kids. It'll be fun. All you got to do is shine my shoes, maybe take out the trash." When the joke didn't make Steve smile, Bucky said, "Come on."

Steve knew Bucky meant well, but he didn't want to impose. "Thank you, Buck, but I can get by on my own."

"The thing is, you don't have to," Bucky said. "I'm with you to the end of the line, pal."

Sam found Steve on top of the dam and knew what he was thinking. "He's gonna be there, you know?"

"I know," Steve said.

"Look, whoever he used to be and the guy he is now, I don't think he's the kind you save. He's the kind you stop."

Steve thought about it. "I don't know if I can do that."

"Well, he might not give you a choice," Sam said. "He doesn't know you."

"He will," Steve said. He believed it. Whatever terrible things had happened to Bucky because of Zola and Hydra, the old Bucky was in there somewhere. Steve had to believe that. "Gear up. It's time."

"You gonna wear that?" Sam asked.

Steve was walking away, down the dam. "No. If you're gonna fight a war, you got to wear a uniform," he said. But he didn't have his Captain America uniform. It was back in the Triskelion. That meant he had a stop to make before everything happened tomorrow.

If he couldn't wear his new uniform, he'd just have to go back to the old one. After all, he knew where to find it.

CHAPTER 31

Alexander Pierce walked the four members of the World Security Council through the Triskelion. It was two hours until Project Insight would launch. Two hours until the dawn of a new world under Hydra control. He wanted them there to see it. "And how was your flight?" he asked, to break the ice.

"Lovely," Councilor Hawley said. "The ride from the airport, less so."

"Sadly, S.H.I.E.L.D. can't control everything," Pierce said.

He'd meant it as a joke, but Councilor Rockwell took the chance to rub Pierce's face in recent events. "Including Captain America."

Pierce let that pass. After today, Captain America wouldn't matter. Neither would S.H.I.E.L.D. or the World Security Council. An aide came up to Pierce with a case containing four identification badges that looked like USB drives. "This facility is biometrically controlled," Pierce said. "And these will give you unrestricted access." They clipped on their badges and he led them toward the elevator.

In the satellite command center, operations techs were shooting the breeze while they waited for the satellite linkup to initialize. "I've been parking there for two months," one of them complained.

"But it's his spot," the other one pointed out.

"So where's he been?"

"I think Afghanistan."

A third tech, who was actually doing her job, talked into a microphone. "Negative, DT6. The pattern is full."

The first tech was still irritated about the parking situation. "Well, he could've said something."

A sharp electronic squeal sounded in their ears. "Ahh!" the first tech said. He tore off his headphones. "Must be the dish. I'll check it out."

When he opened the door to the stairs that led up to the dish array, he was looking at Captain America, Maria Hill, and the Falcon.

"Excuse us," Captain America said. As he stepped aside, the tech noticed that Captain America's suit looked old, not like the new one he had worn in the Battle of New York. It was like something out of a museum. Old-school.

Pierce had some remarks prepared for the councilors, and when they got to his conference room, he began. Once he poured champagne for everyone, that is. This was a big day, and it deserved to be celebrated.

"I know the road hasn't exactly been smooth," he said, "and some of you would have gladly kicked me out of the car along the way. Finally, we're here. And the world should be grateful." He toasted them, and as they tasted their champagne, a voice boomed over the Triskelion's building intercom.

"Attention, all S.H.I.E.L.D. agents. This is Steve Rogers…"

The councilors looked at Pierce in alarm. Pierce set down his drink. Steve Rogers should have been dead. What was he doing in the Triskelion? He thought quickly, keeping his cool in front of the council. So this was how things were going to go, he thought. He'd have to show his cards a little sooner than he'd planned.

Steve spoke into the intercom from the satellite command center. The techs watched from the other side of the room, where Maria Hill had them under guard. "You've heard a lot about me over the last few days. Some of you were even ordered to hunt me down. But I think it's time you know the truth. S.H.I.E.L.D. is not what we thought it was. It's been taken over by Hydra. Alexander Pierce is their leader. The S.T.R.I.K.E. and Insight crew are Hydra as well. I don't know how many more, but I know they're in the building. They could be standing right next to you. They almost have what they want: absolute control. They shot Nick Fury. And it won't end there. If you launch those Helicarriers today, Hydra will be able to kill anyone that stands in their way. Unless we stop them. I know I'm asking a lot. But the price of freedom is high. It always has been. And it's a price I'm willing to pay. And if I'm the only one, then so be it. But I'm willing to bet I'm not."

Sam looked at Steve with admiration when he finished the speech. "Did you write that down first, or was it off the top of your head?"

CHAPTER 32

In the Helicarrier mission control room, the S.T.R.I.K.E. team fanned out to cover exits and critical personnel. Upstairs, other S.T.R.I.K.E. personnel had the World Security Councilors under control. Pierce was in charge. Brock Rumlow walked up to the head launch technician. "Preempt the launch sequence," he ordered. "Send those ships up now."

The tech didn't move. "Is there a problem?" Rumlow asked.

"Um..."

"Is there a problem?" Rumlow repeated, louder this time.

The tech took a deep breath. "I'm sorry, sir. I'm not gonna launch those ships. Captain's orders."

Rumlow drew his gun and pointed it at the technician. "Move away from your station."

A moment later he had a gun to his own head. Holding it was Agent 13, Steve Rogers's neighbor. She looked Rumlow in the eye. "Like he said…"

All around the room, guns appeared as S.H.I.E.L.D. agents drew on the S.T.R.I.K.E. traitors. The air was heavy with the threat of violence.

"Put the gun down!" Agent 13 said. "Captain's orders."

"You picked the wrong side, Agent," Rumlow said.

Her gun didn't waver. "Depends on where you're standing."

Rumlow dropped his gun, watching her carefully. In the brief moment her eyes tracked the gun's fall, he whipped out a knife and cut her across the arm. The room erupted in gunfire, loyal S.H.I.E.L.D. agents against their Hydra infiltrators. The launch tech dove out of the way as Rumlow got his gun back, and with bullets flying around him, Rumlow entered the override sequence. He completed the override before retreating under fire from Agent 13 and the rest of the S.H.I.E.L.D. agents.

Project Insight would begin now.

Three bay doors, each one ten times the size of a football field, opened right at the surface of the Potomac River next to the Triskelion. Inside each bay was a Helicarrier. If those Helicarriers got into the air under Hydra control, the world would be forever changed...and not for the better.

"They're initiating launch," Maria Hill said from the satellite room.

Cap and the Falcon heard her as they ran across the gangway toward the opening launch bay. They could also hear the Helicarriers' huge repulsor engines powering up to full lift capacity. "Hey, Cap, how do we know the good guys from the bad guys?" Falcon asked.

Simple, Cap thought. "If they're shooting at you, they're bad."

Falcon powered up his jetpack and took off as Captain America dropped over the edge of the open bay and landed on the Helicarrier's flight deck. He sprinted down the deck, fighting his way through responding Hydra personnel wearing S.H.I.E.L.D. uniforms. He heard one of the Helicarriers start firing its antiaircraft weapons, and Falcon said, "Hey, Cap, I found those bad guys you were talking about."

Cap looked up and watched Falcon dodging the air bursts. Fireballs and puffs of smoke bloomed in the air all around him. "You okay?"

"I'm not dead yet," Sam said.

Me neither, Cap thought. He kept fighting his way toward the bridge.

Pierce watched the fighting, and something occurred to him. "Let me ask you a question," he asked Councilor Singh, who was from India. "What if Pakistan marched into Mumbai tomorrow and you knew that they were going to drag your daughters into a soccer stadium for execution, and you could just stop it with a flick of the switch? Wouldn't you?" He looked to the councilors, these three men and one woman who could make the next few days much easier if they would just get on board. "Wouldn't you all?" he asked.

Councilor Singh threw his glass to the floor, where it shattered. "Not if it was your switch."

Pierce looked disappointed. He reached back, and a S.T.R.I.K.E. commando handed him a gun. It was time to make a more forceful statement.

But he never got the chance. Councilor Hawley wrenched the gun out of his hand and before he could make another move, she had disabled the S.T.R.I.K.E. guards and had the gun pointed at Pierce. The other councilors stared in amazement—except Yen, who had picked up a dropped S.T.R.I.K.E. sidearm and was also pointing it at Pierce.

They were even more amazed when Hawley touched the side of her face and peeled away a thin mesh, revealing the face of Natasha Romanoff. "I'm sorry," the Black Widow said. "Did I step on your moment?"

CHAPTER 33

They had to get the Helicarriers under their control before they reached three thousand feet, which was when they could link up with the Project Insight satellites. "Falcon, status?" Maria Hill inquired.

"Engaging," he said. He dove through antiaircraft fire from the nearest Helicarrier's deck, trying to get low enough so that the turret barrels couldn't angle down and target him. After a couple near misses he made it, and cleared the deck of Hydra commandos with the pair of submachine guns he had clipped to his jetpack.

He surveyed the deck. Everything was quiet for the moment. "All right, Cap. I'm in."

But he'd spoken too soon. A Quinjet flew around the superstructure and started firing. Falcon turned and zipped away down the flight deck, slaloming under parked Quinjets for cover. One of them exploded, knocking him off balance. He bounced along the flight deck and then dived over it when the Quinjet came in for another pass. Falcon swooped under the Helicarrier, the Quinjet hot on his trail.

On another Helicarrier, Cap was still fighting his way through the Hydra forces. "Eight minutes, Cap," Hill said into his ear.

"Working on it," he answered. He got to the bulkhead door leading into the Helicarrier's command deck and went in, hunting for the main server where the new blades needed to be installed.

Black Widow, still wearing the dress and pearls of a World Security Councilor, worked at an encrypted terminal in Pierce's office. "What are you doing?" one of the councilors asked. The other one still had a gun pointed at Pierce.

"She's disabling security protocols and dumping all the secrets onto the Internet," Pierce explained.

Natasha nodded. "Including Hydra's."

"And S.H.I.E.L.D.'s," he reminded her. "If you do this, none of your past is gonna remain hidden. Are you sure you're ready for the world to see you as you really are?"

She paused just long enough to look him in the eye. "Are you?"

Cap found the server interface in the belly of the Helicarrier. Servers were housed in an open room for good temperature circulation and optimized bandwidth. Helicarriers needed a lot of information going back and forth to keep their command and control systems online. Cap opened up the door containing all the blades and got the new blade slotted into an empty space. Then he closed up the rack of chips and let Hill know. "Alpha lock."

Hill looked at her screen. One of the Helicarriers flashed green. Two more to go. "Falcon, where are you now?"

"I had to take a detour," he called over the sounds of explosions and heavy machine gunfire. He dodged under the Helicarrier again and the Quinjet behind him unleashed a barrage of small missiles. They tracked Falcon in a wide arc until he made a sharp turn back toward the

Helicarrier. The missiles weren't as agile as he was. They exploded along the bottom of the Helicarrier's hull.

One of the missiles, as a matter of fact, blew a hole in just the part of the hull he needed to get in through. "Wooo!" he shouted, and flew in through the smoke and falling wreckage. He landed on the catwalk leading to the server interface. "I'm in." A moment later he had the chip in place, and the whole array locked down again. "Bravo lock," he reported, and dove out through the hole into the open sky again.

"Two down, one to go," Hill said as the second Helicarrier flashed green on her control screen.

On the third Helicarrier, a group of loyal pilots was running out onto the flight deck. "All S.H.I.E.L.D. pilots, scramble," their commanding officer ordered over the pilots' dedicated frequency. "We're the only air support Captain Rogers has got."

As he finished the order, a Quinjet crashed down on the flight deck. The Winter Soldier stepped out of it. The pilots started firing, but he was faster than they were and they weren't trained for small-arms combat. In seconds the Winter Soldier had eliminated most of the flight crew. Two pilots made it to their Quinjets, and the Winter Soldier casually threw a grenade through the closing ramp of one.

As the Quinjet exploded, he jumped up onto the remaining pilot's Quinjet and shot him through the windshield.

Then he got into the Quinjet and took off in it himself.

Captain America would not have any air support after all.

CHAPTER 34

D isabling the encryption is an executive order," Pierce said as Black Widow ran into restricted access on the command terminal. "It takes two alpha level members."

She looked past him, out the window, to the Triskelion's helipad. At that moment a chopper was landing. "Don't worry. Company's coming."

Looking almost good as new, except for one arm in a sling, Nick Fury stepped out of the helicopter and strode into the room.

Pierce, as always, played his politician's charm. "Did you

get my flowers?" he asked. When Fury just looked at him, he said, "I'm glad you're here, Nick."

"Really?" Fury said. "Because I thought you had me killed."

This didn't seem to bother Pierce. "You know how the game works," he said.

"So why make me head of S.H.I.E.L.D.?"

"Because you were the best, and the most ruthless person I ever met."

"I did what I did to protect people."

Pierce smiled a polished smile. "Our enemies are your enemies, Nick. Disorder. War. It's just a matter of time before a dirty bomb goes off in Moscow, or an EMP fries Chicago. Diplomacy? A holding action, Nick. A Band-Aid. And you know where I learned that. Bogotá." He let that sink in. He liked turning Fury's history and methods against him. "You didn't ask. You just did what had to be done."

Fury still didn't say anything. "I can bring order to the lives of seven billion people by sacrificing twenty million," Pierce said, as if it was all a matter of math. "It's the next step, Nick. If you have the courage to take it." By the end of this little speech, Pierce sounded upbeat. Encouraging.

Fury wasn't buying it. "No," he said. "I have the courage not to."

He led Pierce to the security scanner built into one of the walls. Black Widow finished her work at the terminal and picked up her gun again. "Retinal scanner active," a computer voice said.

"You don't think we've wiped your clearance from the system?" Pierce asked. It would need both him and Fury to proceed.

A small smile appeared on Fury's face. "I know you erased my password. Probably deleted my retinal scan. But if you want to stay ahead of me, Mr. Secretary, you need to keep both eyes open." With that, he lifted his eye patch, revealing the scars on his face and the milk-white pupil of his blind eye. He had made sure S.H.I.E.L.D.'s security systems knew both of his eyes...and he had known Pierce wouldn't expect him to have two separate retinal prints in the system. It wasn't easy to outscheme Nick Fury.

The scanner read Pierce's eye, and Fury's. "Alpha level confirmed," the computer voice said. "Encryption code accepted. Safeguards removed."

"Charlie carrier is forty-five degrees off the port bow," Hill informed Captain America. They still needed to get that one under their control.

Hill looked up as two S.T.R.I.K.E. commandos burst through the door. Before they could clear the doorway, she shot them both. "Six minutes," she said.

From the first Helicarrier, Cap called out to Falcon. "Hey, Sam, gonna need a ride."

"Roger," Falcon said. "Let me know when you're ready."

Cap had just jumped off the Helicarrier's flight deck ahead of a series of explosions. "I just did!"

Falcon dove, accelerated, and caught Cap barely a hundred feet from the ground. He powered up his jetpack and got both of them to the flight deck on the third carrier. "You know, you're a lot heavier than you look," he said when they landed.

"I had a big breakfast," Cap said. Right as he said it, the Winter Soldier knocked him over the edge of the deck.

"Steve!" Sam shouted. He spread his wings and dove, but the Winter Soldier caught one wing and threw Sam back onto the flight deck. He jetted straight up, firing at the Winter Soldier, who dove behind a stack of steel crates. That was the break Sam needed. He flew after Steve again—but the Winter Soldier stopped him once more, this time by firing a grappling line that caught his wing. He dragged Sam back onto the carrier and with a powerful jerk he tore off one of Sam's wings.

Then he threw him over the side.

Sam spun crazily in the air. His jetpack sputtered, and he couldn't stay airborne with only one wing. He struggled with a mechanism on the side of the wing harness. The ground rushed toward him with frightening speed. At the last minute he popped the wing loose and a split second later deployed an emergency parachute!

He was so low to the ground that the parachute didn't make for a soft landing, but it did make for a survivable landing. Sam hit the ground hard, at the edge of the Triskelion complex. He staggered to his feet and called out, "Cap! Cap, come in. Are you okay?"

"Yeah, I'm here." Steve was hanging from the edge of a huge thruster nozzle at the rear of the Helicarrier's hull. "I'm still on the Helicarrier. Where are you?"

"I'm grounded," Sam said. He was frustrated to be letting his team down. "The suit's down. Sorry, Cap."

"Don't worry. I got it," Cap said. Above him, the Winter Soldier peered over the hull but couldn't see Cap from where he was. After a long look, he headed back up the flight deck.

Okay, Cap thought. *We still have a chance.*

CHAPTER 35

Emergency evacuation alerts blared throughout the Triskelion complex. On one of the upper levels, Brock Rumlow was trying to rejoin the remaining members of the S.T.R.I.K.E. force. "All personnel, proceed to designated safety zones," an automated voice said over the loudspeakers. "All S.H.I.E.L.D. agents regroup at rally point Delta."

"Sir," one of Rumlow's men said in his ear. "The council's been breached."

How was that possible? Pierce had all the biometric

security protocols in place. "Repeat, dispatch," Rumlow said.

"Black Widow's up there."

"Headed up." Gun in hand, he went toward the stairs.

On a surveillance camera, Maria Hill saw him. "Falcon?" She had seen him lose his wings, but he was close enough to help.

"Yeah," he answered.

"Rumlow's headed for the council."

He looked up, figuring the quickest way to get there. "I'm on it."

In the server interface dome on the bottom level of Charlie carrier, Captain America walked along the catwalk leading to the racks where the server blades were installed. He walked slowly. It wouldn't help to rush, because between him and the racks stood Bucky Barnes— the Winter Soldier.

He stopped about twenty feet from Bucky. "People are gonna die, Buck. I can't let that happen."

Bucky stared back at him. There was no recognition or emotion on his face.

Steve gave it one last try. "Please don't make me do this."

Still Bucky didn't move. Steve thought of what Fury

had said, about the things you had to do sometimes for the greater good. To protect people. If Bucky didn't move, millions of people were going to die.

And if Bucky wasn't going to move on his own, Steve would just have to make him.

He flung his shield and Bucky deflected it with his cybernetic arm, just as Steve had anticipated. Catching the shield as he rushed Bucky, Steve blocked three quick gunshots and hit Bucky hard enough to make him stagger and drop his gun. Bucky sprawled on his back next to the racks, which were in a column that descended from the ceiling of the upside-down dome. He sprang to his feet with a knife in hand. Cap was ready, blocking knife thrusts and knocking Bucky out of the way. He got into the small space with the server rack, but he only had time to pull one of the blades loose before Bucky came after him again. He stopped a punch from Bucky's cybernetic arm and they wrestled back out onto the catwalk. Both of them fell over the railing onto a lower level, skidding on the angled floor. Steve dropped the server blade and it slid to the edge and over a long drop to the bottom of the dome. He would have to go past Bucky to get it.

Bucky knocked him down and the server blade slid off into space. Steve and Bucky, still fighting, tumbled after it.

A soft beep came from the Triskelion terminal. "Done," Black Widow said. She looked at her phone. "And it's trending."

Fury and Pierce looked at each other. This would change everything. Pierce looked at his own phone and acted as if he were interested in what social media might be saying about him. But he was looking at a different icon on his screen. He touched it three times in quick succession, and the three members of the World Security Council dropped to the floor.

Black Widow and Fury both had their weapons on him, but he still had his thumb ready over his phone screen. "Unless you want a two-inch hole in your sternum, I'd put that gun down," he said. He nodded at the biometric badge. That was armed the moment you pinned it on."

Fury and Natasha lowered their firearms. It seemed Pierce's game wasn't quite over yet.

Steve was almost to the server blade when his own shield knocked him down: Bucky had found Cap's shield before he did and threw it. It fell nearby and Steve dove to pick it up as Bucky emptied his pistol, bullets ricocheting all over the dome. They fought across the bottom of the glass dome, nearly three thousand feet of air between them and the ground. Bucky grasped the server blade and Steve put him in an armlock. He twisted Bucky's arm, hating to do it but knowing how many lives were at risk. Bucky cried out in pain.

"Drop it!" Steve shouted. All he wanted was the blade. He didn't want to hurt Bucky.

But Bucky wouldn't drop it. He tried to hit Steve with his cybernetic arm until Steve got it in a leg lock. He wrapped his arm around Bucky's throat and squeezed. "Drop it!" he shouted again.

Bucky fought, but in the chokehold he couldn't keep his grip for long. His hand relaxed, and his eyes rolled up in his head. The server blade fell free. Steve let Bucky go. His old friend rolled over limp as Steve grabbed the server blade and ran.

CHAPTER 36

I'm on forty-one, headed toward the southwest stairwell,"
Rumlow reported to his Hydra dispatch command.
He had to cross the main floor to get to the stairwell that
would lead to the top floor.

As he walked out into the room, a punch from his blind
side knocked him flat. He looked up and saw Sam Wilson.
"This is gonna hurt," Rumlow said as he got to his feet.
"There are no prisoners with Hydra."

"Man, shut up," Sam said. They charged each other,
both men knowing that whoever made it through would
tip the balance upstairs.

"One minute," Maria Hill said as Cap climbed the column toward the server blade racks at the top. Cap was about to answer, when Bucky started shooting at him from below. One of the bullets caught him in the leg and another sparked off the column near his head. Part of Steve was glad he hadn't killed Bucky, but he knew he would regret it if Charlie Helicarrier got its weapons deployed and Hydra completed their twisted version of Project Insight.

He struggled on, getting to the top level just as Maria Hill said, "Thirty seconds, Cap."

"Stand by," he said. He got the server blade from his belt and reached for the empty slot.

That was when the Winter Soldier shot him right through the stomach.

Cap sank to the floor, all the strength gone from his legs. "Charlie..." he gasped. He couldn't move.

But he had to.

He heard the voices of the Hydra crew talking to one another over their open frequency. "We've reached three thousand feet.... Satellite link coming online now. We are go to target."

Steve forced himself to lean forward. He tried to get

one foot under him. "Target saturation reached," one of the Hydra techs said. "All targets assigned." That would be millions of people. All three Helicarriers were still under Hydra control.

Because Captain America had failed.

No, Steve thought. *That's not how this ends.* He got up to one knee.

"Fire when ready," the Hydra deck officer said.

"Firing in...three, two..."

Steve was leaning on the edge of the server blade rack. With the blade in his fingers, he reached toward the empty slot.

"One..."

The blade snapped into place. Steve collapsed back to the floor. "Charlie...lock," he panted.

Over the comm frequency he heard the Hydra officers. "Where are the targets? Where are the targets?"

You're about to find out, Steve thought. Maria Hill had programmed the blades to turn the Helicarriers on each other. Where before there had been nearly a million targets, now there would be only three. No more Project Insight. No more Hydra. No more S.H.I.E.L.D.

Also no more Captain America if he couldn't get moving. "Okay, Cap, get out of there," Hill said.

Easier said than done, he thought. He wasn't going anywhere. The wound in his gut was too bad. "Fire now," he said.

"But, Steve..."

"Do it! Do it now!" He hadn't come this far to have the whole thing fail because he couldn't get out in time.

Without another word, Maria Hill entered the command.

The three Helicarriers opened up fire on one another with cannons and missiles and smaller weapons. It was a barrage unlike anything ever seen before. Each Helicarrier was as powerful as an entire navy all by itself, and as they started to destroy one another in the skies over Washington, DC, Alexander Pierce looked out the window and said, "What a waste."

"So, you still on the fence about Rogers's chances?" Fury asked him.

Pierce wouldn't look at Fury. He gestured at Natasha instead. "Time to go, Councilwoman. This way. Come on. You're going to fly me out of here."

"You know, there was a time I would've taken a bullet for you," Fury said.

"You already did," Pierce said with a grin. "You will again, when it's useful."

While neither of them was paying attention to her, Natasha pulled one of the small disks out of her pocket, a disk like the one she had used to disable the Winter Soldier's arm. She activated it by jabbing it into her lapel, near the biometric badge. Electricity arced all across her torso and she collapsed—but Pierce no longer had a lethal threat.

Fury didn't waste any time. He knew immediately what had happened, and while Pierce was still staring at his phone, Fury picked up his gun and shot him twice through the chest. Pierce dropped without a word.

Fury knelt next to Natasha. "Romanoff. Natasha. Natasha! Come on!" He couldn't tell how badly she was hurt.

Her eyelids fluttered. "Ow," she said. "Those really do sting."

He helped her to her feet and they ran for Fury's chopper. Behind them, as he died, Alexander Pierce's last words were a whisper. "Hail Hydra..."

CHAPTER 37

utside, the Helicarriers continued to blast one another out of the sky. One of them heeled over into a dive and crashed into another. They both plowed into the river, crushing the launch bay on the upstream side and tearing themselves to pieces with the force of their impact.

The third Helicarrier, out of control, began to tip toward the upper floors of the Triskelion itself. It started to tear into the forty-first floor just as Brock Rumlow was looking at the bloodied Sam Wilson and saying, "You're out of your depth, kid."

Sam looked over Rumlow's shoulder and saw what was

about to happen. Then he ran. He ran as fast as Steve Rogers had that morning on the National Mall. Faster, even. As Brock Rumlow disappeared in the collapsing wreckage behind him, Sam ran faster than he ever had in his life. "Please tell me you got that chopper in the air!" he shouted into his comm.

Natasha came right back. "Sam, where are you?"

"Forty-first floor! Northwest corner!"

"We're on it! Stay where you are!"

"Not an option!" he yelled, and dove out the window.

Nick Fury was one of the best helicopter pilots around. Even so, catching someone in midair was no easy trick. You had to tip the chopper hard to one side to keep the falling person away from the rotor blades. Then you had to tip it back fast enough that you didn't lose lift. Also, you had to do those things with enough speed that the falling person didn't go right into the chopper and out the other door.

Fury had never done it before, but lucky for Sam Wilson, he got it right on the first try. Sam had only fallen a few floors when Fury picked him out of the sky. The chopper wheeled around and maneuvered out of the crashing Helicarrier's way as it plowed through the rest of the Triskelion.

"Forty-first floor! Forty-first!" Sam shouted. He felt like he'd fallen a long way.

"It's not like they put the floor numbers on the outside of the building," Fury said.

"Hill!" Natasha called. "Where's Steve? You got a location on Rogers?" She was looking at the Helicarrier. It wasn't going to be in the air much longer.

In the shattered wreckage of Charlie Helicarrier's server interface dome, Steve Rogers used all of his strength to lift a fallen steel beam off Bucky Barnes. The Helicarrier was going to crash, and before that happened, Steve was going to make sure he had his say. *To the end of the line*, Bucky had said to him once. Steve owed him the same.

Barnes rolled free and glared at him but didn't attack right away. "You know me," Steve said.

"No, I don't!" Barnes screamed, and threw a punch that knocked Steve down. He hadn't tried to block it. Maybe he couldn't have even if he tried. The wounds in his stomach and leg had left him weak.

Steve got up anyway. He didn't have much left, but he wasn't going to give up on his old friend. "Bucky. You've known me your whole life."

Bucky knocked him down again. The Helicarrier

drifted lower. It would crash soon. "Your name is James Buchanan Barnes."

"Shut up!" Bucky hit him again.

Steve got to his feet one last time and dropped his shield through a hole in the dome. It fell away, curving down toward the river. "I'm not gonna fight you," he said. "You're my friend."

Bucky tackled him and started punching him. "You're my mission. You're my mission!" He said it over and over again, and hit Steve over and over again, but Steve didn't fight back. Eventually Bucky stopped. There was a strange look on his face. "You're my mission."

"Then finish it," Steve said. "Because I'm with you to the end of the line."

Something happened to Bucky's expression. Steve thought maybe he understood, but he was too beat-up to say anything else. The Helicarrier came apart around them then, and the last thing Steve remembered was falling.

He woke up with Sam Wilson sitting at his bedside and Marvin Gaye's *Trouble Man* playing on his phone. "On your left," Steve rasped. Sam glanced over at him and grinned.

CHAPTER 38

atasha Romanoff was called to testify before Congress, because she was the only agent they could find. Steve was still in the hospital. Fury had disappeared. Hill had gone into the private sector, with some help from Tony Stark. So it was up to Natasha to take the congressional heat. They swore her in and then got right to the grilling.

"Why haven't we yet heard from Captain Rogers?" one of the representatives wanted to know. She had already told them that destroying the Helicarriers was Captain America's plan, but they wanted to hear it from him.

"I don't know what there is left for him to say," she said.

"I think the wreck in the middle of the Potomac made his point fairly eloquently." *Also*, she thought, *he's in the hospital.*

"Well, he could explain how this country is expected to maintain its national security now that he and you have laid waste to our intelligence apparatus," a general said. Natasha knew he was one of the Joint Chiefs, and that he had ties she considered suspicious.

"Hydra was selling you lies, not intelligence," she said.

"Many of which you seemed to have had a personal hand in telling," the general shot back. "Agent, you should know that there are some on this committee who feel, given your service record, both for this country and against it, that you belong in a penitentiary. Not mouthing off on Capitol Hill."

All right, Natasha thought. *It's time to set them straight.* "You're not going to put me in a prison. You're not going to put any of us in a prison. You know why?"

"Do enlighten us," said a congressman.

"Because you need us. Yes, the world is a vulnerable place, and yes, we help make it that way. But we're also the ones best qualified to defend it. So, if you want to arrest me, arrest me. You'll know where to find me."

She got up and walked out then, knowing they wouldn't

arrest her. Because she was right. Flashbulbs popped, reporters shouted, and Natasha Romanoff ignored it all. It was time to plan what they were all going to do now that S.H.I.E.L.D. wasn't going to be around anymore.

Fury got word to Steve and Sam that they should meet in a cemetery—by his own tombstone, as a matter of fact. When they were all together, Fury said, "So, you've experienced this sort of thing before."

Cap nodded. "You get used to it." It would be easier on Fury because he wouldn't have to deal with the loss of seventy years.

"We've been data mining Hydra's files," Fury said. "Looks like a lot of rats didn't go down with the ship. I'm headed to Europe tonight. Wanted to ask if you'd come."

"There's something I got to do first," Steve said.

"How about you, Wilson? Could use a man with your abilities."

"I'm more of a soldier than a spy," Sam said.

"All right, then." Fury shook their hands. "Anybody asks for me, tell them they can find me right here."

"You should be honored," Natasha said as Fury walked away. "That's about as close as he gets to saying thank you."

"Not going with him?" Steve asked.

"No."

This surprised him a little. "Not staying here?"

"Nah." Natasha shook her head. "I blew all my covers. I got to go figure out a new one."

"That might take a while," he said.

She nodded. "I'm counting on it."

They all needed a break, Steve thought. But it seemed like the bad guys never took one.

"That thing you asked for, I called in a few favors from Kiev," Natasha said. She handed him a folder from Russian intelligence: their dossier on Bucky Barnes. Steve figured Bucky must be alive. Someone had pulled him out of the river. Who else could it have been?

"Will you do me a favor?" Natasha asked. "Call that nurse."

"She's not a nurse."

"And you're not a S.H.I.E.L.D. agent."

"What was her name again?"

"Sharon. She's nice." She kissed him on the cheek and turned to go. Then she stopped and glanced back at the folder. "Be careful, Steve. You might not want to pull on that thread."

He opened the folder and saw a photograph of Bucky. Then he noticed Sam standing next to him. "You're going after him," Sam said. It wasn't a question.

"You don't have to come with me."

"I know." Sam paused. "When do we start?"

TURN THE PAGE FOR AN EXCITING PREVIEW OF

MARVEL CINEMATIC UNIVERSE
PHASE TWO

CHAPTER 1

The twins knew something was wrong. They reached for each other and touched hands, wondering what they should do. Around them, alarms and sirens blared. They heard explosions from outside the Leviathan Chamber. Soldiers ran to take up defensive positions. Before them, the scepter stood in its housing, the blue energy from its gem crackling in the air above it.

The Avengers charged through a snowy forest toward the fortress that was their target, at the edge of the city of Sokovia. Enemy soldiers fired at them. Hawkeye located one of the soldiers' firing positions and blew it up with an explosive arrow. Thor smashed another gunner's nest with his hammer. The soldiers inside tumbled out, falling out of the tree. Hulk took on the heavy equipment, smashing a tank and looking around for another one.

Zooming overhead, Iron Man crashed hard into an invisible energy shield protecting the fortress. He swore as he tumbled to the ground.

"Language, Stark," Captain America said. "Jarvis, what's the view from upstairs?"

Jarvis was feeding information into the displays inside Iron Man's helmet. "It appears the central building is protected by some kind of energy shield. Strucker's use of alien technology is well beyond that of any other HYDRA base we've taken down."

All the other Avengers could hear him because of their communication devices on a secure team-only wavelength.

"Loki's scepter must be there," Thor said. "Strucker couldn't have mounted this defense without it. At long last…"

"At long last is lasting a little long, boys," Black Widow said.

"Yeah," Hawkeye commented from behind a tree, where he was picking off HYDRA soldiers one after another. "I think we're losing the element of surprise."

Soldiers poured out of the fortress, lining its exterior walls and counterattacking. The Avengers were closer to it now. On the other side of the fortress was the city. Iron Man soared over the fortress. He couldn't get through the energy shield protecting the main keep, but the soldiers on the walls were outside the shield. He fired repulser beams at them and dodged their return fire. Some of them had Chitauri weapons.

In the forest, racing toward the fortress, the rest of the Avengers fought Strucker's troops. Captain America skidded to a halt on his motorcycle and threw it at a jeep. The jeep swerved and crashed into a tree.

Inside the fortress, Baron Strucker strode through the command center, looking for the officer on duty. "Who gave the order to attack?"

The soldier nearest him stammered, "Herr Strucker, it's...it's the Avengers."

Another soldier, more calmly, added, "They landed in the far woods. The perimeter guard panicked."

"They have to be after the scepter," Strucker said. "Can we hold them?"

"They're the Avengers!" the first soldier said, as if he couldn't believe the question.

The Avengers, Strucker thought. *Everyone fears them.* "Deploy the rest of the tanks," he ordered a waiting officer. "Concentrate fire on the weak ones. A hit may make them close ranks." He turned to a scientist accompanying him, Dr. List. "Everything we've accomplished...we're on the verge of our greatest breakthrough!"

"Then let's show them what we've accomplished," Dr. List answered smoothly. "Send out the twins."

"It's too soon."

"It's what they signed up for," Dr. List pointed out.

Strucker shook his head, watching the soldiers deploy out of the command center. "My men can hold them," he said, but inside he wasn't sure.

CHAPTER 2

A heavy Chitauri gun fired at Iron Man. The beam missed him and destroyed part of a building in Sokovia. "Sir, the city is taking fire," Jarvis said.

"Strucker's not going to worry about civilian casualties," Tony said. "Send in the Iron Legion."

The Iron Legion was a squadron of remotely operated Iron Man armored suits. They landed in different parts of Sokovia. "Please return to your homes," one said. "We will do our best to ensure your safety during this engagement."

In another part of the city, another Iron Legionnaire broadcast its recorded speech. "This quadrant is unsafe.

Please back away. We wish to avoid collateral damage and will inform you when the current conflict is resolved. We are here to help."

Not all the Sokovians loved the Avengers. One of them threw a bottle of acid at the Iron Legionnaire. It smashed on the legionnaire's mask, melting partway through it.

Tony got a damage report from the legionnaire. *What ingrates*, he thought. Then he had to dodge incoming fire and decided the legionnaires were on their own.

Strucker rallied his troops, knowing the Avengers would eventually breach the fortress's defenses. "Once again, the West bring violence to your country! Your homes! But they will learn the price of their arrogance! We will not yield. The American send their circus freaks to test us, and we will send them back in bags! No surrender!"

The men cheered as Strucker turned and spoke quietly to Dr. List. "I'm going to surrender. Delete everything. If we give the Avengers the scepter, they may not look too far into what we've been doing with it."

"But the twins," Dr. List protested.

"They're not ready to take on—"

Dr. List pointed. "No, I mean...the twins."

Strucker turned to see where Dr. List was pointing. A moment ago, the twins had been waiting, together as always, near the scepter in a shadowed corner of the room.

Now they were gone.

Hawkeye dodged the crackling blue beams of the Chitauri weapons, finding cover behind a tree. He rolled out and fired at one of the defending gunners.

The arrow disappeared. What the—?

He drew his bow again and was about to let fly when something hit him hard enough to knock him sprawling back into the trees. He got up ready to fight, and for a split second a man appeared in front of him, wearing a close-fitting blue suit, with a shock of white hair. The man held up Clint's arrow.

"You didn't see that coming?" he said mockingly. Then, before Hawkeye could respond, the man vanished.

No, not vanished. Ran at an incredible speed. For just a moment, Hawkeye had seen him start to move.

In the moment he spent thinking about that, a blast tore through his side. He spun and went down hard.

"Clint!" Black Widow called. "Clint's hit."

Captain America ran to Hawkeye's aid and was knocked hard out of the way, slamming into a tree trunk. He looked around and called out, "We've got an Enhanced in the field!" That was their term for other people like the Avengers, who had some kind of power unknown to regular humans.

Black Widow got to Hawkeye's side. "Can someone take out that bunker?" She ducked away from incoming fire.

The Hulk was the first to respond, plowing through the bunker and destroying it. "Thank you," Black Widow said. She looked down at Hawkeye's wound. It was bad.

"Stark, we really need to get inside," Captain America said. The invisible shield was holding them up, and they still didn't know where the Enhanced was or what he could do.

"I'm closing in," Iron Man said. A Chitauri beam knocked him off balance in the air. "Jarvis, am I closing in? You see a power source for that shield?"

He landed on the outside wall of the fortress, knocking soldiers away as Jarvis responded, "There's a dense particle wave below the north tower."

"Great," Iron Man said. He fired repulsors down a

narrow alley, blasting open a gate. "I want to poke it with something."

Taking to the air again, he concentrated his fire on the shield in that area. A rupture appeared, and the shield began to lose coherence. The hole got larger, energy spitting around its edge. They were through!

"Drawbridge is down, people!" Iron Man called out.

Captain America heard him and turned to Thor, who was finishing off the closest defending soldiers. "The Enhanced?" Thor asked.

"He's a blur," Cap said. "All the new players we've faced, I've never seen this." He scanned the woods and the outside of the fort. "Actually, I still haven't."

"Clint's hit pretty bad, guys," Black Widow said over their comm link. "We're gonna need evac."

More tanks and soldiers started spilling from the fortress gate. "I'll get Barton to the jet," Thor said. The sooner we're gone, the better. You and Stark secure the scepter."

"Copy that," Cap said. Soldiers charged out from their cover, with a tank coming up behind them. All of them were in a single line because of how thick the forest was in their area. "It's like they're lining up," Thor said.

Cap knew what he was getting at. "Well, they're excited," he said.

He held out his shield, and Thor swung Mjolnir against it, sending a shock wave down the path that scattered the soldiers and destroyed the tank. They'd practiced that move, and both of them grinned to see it work.

Thor began spinning his hammer, getting ready to take off. "Find the scepter!" he called.

"And for God's sake, watch your language," Iron Man added.

Cap headed for the fortress. He couldn't help but smile at Tony's joke. "That's not going away anytime soon."

CHAPTER 3

With the shield down, Iron Man could fly straight through the fortress's large windows into what looked like a command center. The soldiers inside hit him with everything they had, mostly machine guns, but they couldn't hurt the suit. "Let's talk this over," Tony said, holding up his arms...then he took every single one of them out with a burst of disabling fire from his shoulder guns. He nodded, surveying what he had done. "Good talk."

Most of the soldiers weren't in any shape to reply, but one of them groaned. "No it wasn't."

Grinning, Tony moved deeper into the fortress. He

found a scientist busy at a computer terminal in another room and leveled him with a repulsor blast. Then he looked at the computer and opened the Iron Man armor to get out of it. "Sentry mode," he said. Then he pulled out a small device and set it next to the computer. It lit up and started copying all the data from the terminal. "Okay, Jarvis, you know I want it all. Make sure you copy Hill at HQ."

Outside, two legionnaires carried Hawkeye on a stretcher as Black Widow watched. "We're all locked down out here," she said. The rest of the soldiers were surrendering, with Thor making sure they didn't get any ideas about further resistance.

Captain America was going inside. "Then get to Banner," he said. "It's time for a lullaby." The Hulk was a powerful ally, but he could also be dangerous. Black Widow had the best rapport with him and was the best at getting him to turn back into Bruce Banner.

Back at the computer terminal, Tony was looking around. "He's got to be hiding more than data," he said out loud. "Jarvis, give me an IR scan." Maybe something would show up on infrared that Tony couldn't see.

"The wall to your left," Jarvis said. "I'm reading steel reinforcement...and an air current."

Tony looked more closely. There was a tiny line in the wall. He followed it with his fingertips, looking... "Please be a secret door, please be a secret door..."

With a click, the door slid aside.

"Yay," Tony said. On the other side of the doorway was a long, dark stairway. He headed down.

Black Widow found the Hulk tearing apart the remains of an enemy tank. She approached carefully and sat where he could see her. "Hey, big guy," she said. "Sun's getting real low."

The Hulk stopped what he was doing and scowled at her. She held out one hand, palm up. He hesitated, then did the same. Natasha ran her fingers softly over his palm and up the inside of his wrist. She felt the tensions simmering in every fiber of the Hulk's muscles. He sighed and pulled away from her, walking slowly—and his change started. He shrank and the green color vanished from his skin. By the time he reached the other side of the clearing from the destroyed tank, he was Bruce Banner again, staring into space as he recovered from the change. Natasha found a blanket and put it over him. She was the only Avenger who could do this. It had started to mean a lot to her. Bruce was still haunted by some of the things he'd done while he was the Hulk, and it made Natasha feel better to know that he trusted her. She waited with him and also for word from inside Baron Strucker's fortress.

Captain America punched his way through the fortress garrison until he caught Strucker trying to escape deeper into the maze of passages and rooms. "Baron Strucker," Cap said. "HYDRA's number one thug."

"Technically, I'm a thug for S.H.I.E.L.D.," Strucker said.

"Well, then, technically you're unemployed," Cap shot back. "Where's Loki's scepter?"

"Don't worry, I'll give you the precious scepter. I know when I'm beat. You'll mention how I cooperated, I hope?"

"I'll put it right under 'illegal human experimentation,'" Cap said, referring to the Enhanced they had seen outside. "How many are there?"

Strucker was looking over his shoulder, a sudden smile on his face. Cap turned to see a young woman coming out of the shadows. She was slim and alluring, but also strange, her eyes wide and not quite focused on him. There was definitely something off about her. He had just completed that thought when she flicked her wrist and sent him flying without ever touching him. He rolled down a flight of stairs, his shield absorbing some of the impact. By the time he'd gotten to his feet and raced back into the room, she was gone. A heavy vault door ground shut behind her.

"We've got a second Enhanced," he warned the team. "Female. Do not engage."

Strucker was gloating. "You're going to have to move faster than that if—"

Captain America was out of patience. He knocked Strucker into the wall and considered what to do next.

Coming out of the tunnel at the bottom of the secret staircase, Tony Stark found himself in a huge chamber littered with equipment. He was still taking it all in when Cap's voice came over the comm link. "Guys, I got Strucker."

"Yeah," Tony said. "I got...something bigger."

Suspended from the ceiling was a Chitauri Leviathan. The last time Tony had seen one of them, it had been trying to destroy New York City. He looked up at it, then got himself focused on the lab equipment again. There were prototype weapons, some robotic components, strange bio-tech assemblies...it would take him some time to figure out what all of it was.

And there, set into a pedestal with cables and conduits running out of it, was Loki's scepter. "Thor," Tony said into the comm. "I got eyes on the prize."

He started toward the scepter, looking closely at it to see if it was defended in some way. He was so focused on it that he never saw the woman next to him, whispering in his ear as red tendrils of magical energy wormed out from her fingertips and into his mind.

Tony turned and saw the Leviathan, whole and roaring over him. He was in an alien landscape, the sky overhead thick with stars. There were bodies everywhere, soldiers in strange uniforms...and the Avengers. Thor, Black Widow, the Hulk, Captain America. All dead. Cap was closest. Still eyeing the Leviathan, Tony knelt to see if Cap still bore any signs of life—and Cap's arm shot out! He grabbed Tony. "You could have saved us. Why? Why didn't you do more? We could have... saved..."

Cap's hand fell away, and he died.

Tony looked up and saw not one Leviathan but ten, then a hundred, surrounded by an endless fleet of alien vessels, all lifting off from this dead planet and heading for Earth, which hung like a shining blue marble in distant space...

Tony snapped out of it, dropping to his knees, sweat pouring down his face from the intensity of the vision. What had happened to him? Must have been a flashback from the Battle of New York. He looked back to the scepter. All their problems had started there, and once the Avengers had the scepter, those problems would be over. He reached out and took Loki's scepter.

From the shadows, the twins watched. "We're just going to let him take it?" the man asked quietly.

His sister nodded, a wicked smile on her face. She had a plan.

CHAPTER 4

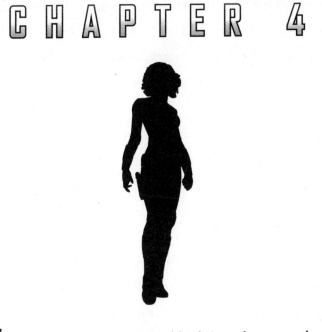

The Avengers' Quinjet soared high into the atmosphere, headed from Sokovia back to base. Tony was in the pilot's chair. Behind him, Hawkeye lay on a chair folded down as a makeshift gurney. Thor, Black Widow, and Captain America watched over him. He was in rough shape. Behind them all, Bruce sat by himself.

Natasha went back to him, knowing she could do nothing for Clint right then. "Hey," she said. "The lullaby worked better than ever."

Bruce still looked worried. "I wasn't expecting a Code

Green." That was what they had started calling his transformations into the Hulk.

"If you hadn't been there, there would have been double the casualties. And my best friend would have been a treasured memory."

"You know, sometimes exactly what I want to hear isn't exactly what I want to hear," Bruce said.

Natasha considered this. She spent a lot of time trying to help Bruce, but sometimes she thought he didn't want to be helped. "How long before you trust me?"

He looked up at her. "It's not you I don't trust."

Their gazes met. She was really starting to care for him, and she knew he felt the same. "Thor!" she said. This would help. "Report on the Hulk?"

"The gates of Hel are filled with the screams of his victims!" Thor said proudly. She shot him a glare, and he realized his mistake. "But not the screams of the dead," he added quickly. "Wounded screams, mainly. Whimpering. A great roar of complaining, and tales of sprained, uh... deltoids. And gout."

Bruce and Natasha looked at each other again, smiling now at Thor's awkwardness.

"Banner," Tony said from the pilot's chair. "Dr. Cho's on her way from Seoul. Okay if she sets up in your lab?"

Bruce nodded. "She knows her way around."

More quietly, Tony consulted with Jarvis. "Tell her to prep everything. Barton's going to need the full treatment."

"Very good, sir," Jarvis said. "Approach vector is locked."

"Jarvis, take the wheel," Tony said. He spun in his chair and went back to Thor, who sat with the scepter wrapped in a cloth. None of them wanted to touch it bare-handed.

"Feels good, right?" Tony prompted. "You've been after this thing since S.H.I.E.L.D. collapsed. Not that I haven't enjoyed our little raiding parties, but..."

"But this brings it to a close," Thor said.

Cap joined them. "As soon as we find out what else that thing's been used for. And I don't just mean weapons. Since when is Strucker capable of human enhancement?"

"Banner and I will give it the once-over before it goes back to Asgard," Tony said. To Thor, he added, "Cool with you. Just a few days until the farewell party. You're staying, right?"

"Of course," Thor said. "A victory should be honored with revels."

"Well, hopefully this puts an end to the Chitauri and HYDRA," Cap said. "So, yes. Revels."

Around sunset the Quinjet arced over New York City and braked to a landing on the new pad on top of Avengers Tower. Tony had rebuilt the building after the Battle of New York, and it was better than ever. No longer just Stark Tower, now it was the headquarters and research center for the Avengers.

Maria Hill met them on the landing pad. As Thor and the others went with Hawkeye to the lab for his treatment, Cap and Tony stayed with Agent Hill. "Dr. Cho's all set up, boss," she said to Tony.

He nodded toward Captain America. "He's the boss. I just pay for everything, design everything, and make everyone look cooler."

"What's the word on Strucker?" Cap asked.

"NATO's got him," Hill said. The European military authorities would hold him until they decided what to do.

"And the two Enhanced?"

She handed Cap a file. He looked at it and saw two pictures, one of each of the Enhanced they had seen in the Sokovian fortress. They had been photographed at a political rally protesting American involvement in Sokovia. "Wanda and Pietro Maximoff," she said. "Twins, orphaned at ten, when a shell collapsed their apartment building. Sokovia's had a rough history. It's nowhere special, but it's on the way to everywhere special."

Cap took this in. He was more interested in people than geopolitics. "Their abilities?"

"He's got increased metabolism and improved thermal homeostasis. Her thing is neuroelectric interface. Telekinesis, mind control..."

He was looking at her the way he always did when she used specialized vocabulary.

"He's fast and she's weird," Hill said to keep it simple.

Cap nodded. "They're going to show up again."

"Agreed," Hill said. "File says they volunteered for Strucker's experiments. It's nuts."

"Yeah," Cap said. "What kind of monster lets a German scientist experiment on them to protect their country?"

He watched her get his joke. That was exactly what Steve Rogers had done during World War II. "We're not at war, Captain," Hill said.

"They are," Cap answered.

Tony got repairs started on the damaged Iron Legionnaires, checked on Hawkeye, and then met Bruce outside the lab. "How's he doing?" Bruce asked.

"Unfortunately, he's still Barton," Tony said. "He's fine. He's thirsty."

Bruce went to join Dr. Cho at Hawkeye's bedside. Tony turned his attention to the scepter, which he had put into a device specially designed to hold it for analysis. "Look alive, Jarvis. It's playtime. We've got only a couple of days with this joystick, so let's make the most of it. How we doing with the structural and compositional analysis?"

"The scepter is alien," Jarvis responded. "There are elements I can't quantify."

"So there are elements you can?"

"The jewel appears to be a protective housing for something inside," Jarvis said. "Something very powerful."

"Like a reactor?"

"Like a computer. I believe I'm deciphering code."

Huh, Tony thought. *That's a new wrinkle.* He dug into the problem and lost track of time.

CHAPTER 5

In Bruce's part of the lab, they had set up a makeshift medical facility. Bruce and Dr. Cho stayed busy, with help from some of Dr. Cho's lab assistants, while Natasha watched. "He's really okay?" Natasha asked. "Pretending to need this guy really brings the team together."

Clint rolled his eyes at the joke.

"There's no possibility of deterioration," Dr. Cho said as she monitored one of the machines working on Clint. "The nano-molecular functionality is instantaneous. His cells don't know they're bonding with simulacra."

Translating Dr. Cho's medical jargon, Bruce said, "She's creating tissue."

"If I had him in my lab, the regeneration cradle could do it in twenty minutes," Dr. Cho said.

Tony came in. "He's flatlining, call it. Time?"

Clint smiled weakly. "I'm gonna live forever. I'm gonna be made of plastic."

Tony handed him a drink. "Here's your beverage."

"You'll be made of you, Mr. Barton," Dr. Cho said. "Your own girlfriend won't be able to tell the difference."

"I don't have a girlfriend."

"That, I can't fix," Dr. Cho said. She turned to Tony. "This is the next thing, Tony. Your clunky metal suits are going to be left in the dust."

"That is exactly the plan," Tony said. "And, Helen, I expect to see you at the party Saturday."

"Unlike you, I don't have a lot of time for parties." She looked down at a chart her assistant handed her and added, "Will... Thor be there?"

Tony and Bruce exchanged a look. Everyone had a crush on Thor. Tony nodded toward the door, and Bruce followed him back to Tony's lab. "What's the rumpus?" Bruce asked as they entered.

"Well, the scepter," Tony said. "We were wondering

how Strucker got so inventive. I've been analyzing the gem inside. Now you may recognize…"

He swept his hands over the holographic display near the scepter, and a computer matrix appeared. It was orange and yellow, arranged in a pattern of straight lines and symbols just as Tony had designed it.

"Jarvis," Bruce said.

"Doctor," Jarvis said, returning the greeting.

"When we started out, Jarvis was just a natural-language UI," Tony said, meaning user interface. "Now he runs more of the business than anyone besides Pepper, including the Iron Legion. Top of the line."

"I suspect not for long," Jarvis said.

"Yeah," Tony agreed. "Meet the competition."

He gestured at the display again, and another matrix appeared. It was larger than Jarvis, blue instead of orange, and it had hundreds of interconnected nodes for every one in Jarvis's matrix. This was what the scepter contained. "It's beautiful," Bruce said.

"What does it look like it's doing?" Tony asked him.

"Like it's thinking," Bruce said. "This could be a…not a human mind, but…" He pointed at some of the nodes. "You see these? Like neurons firing."

"Down in Strucker's lab, I saw some fairly advanced

robotics work. They deep-sixed the data, but I'm guessing he was knocking on a very particular door."

"Artificial intelligence," Bruce said.

"This could be it, Bruce. This could be the key to creating Ultron."

Bruce looked at Tony. "I thought Ultron was a fantasy."

"Yesterday it was," Tony said. "But if we can harness this power . . . apply it to the Iron Legion protocol . . ."

"That's a man-size if."

"Our job is if. What if you were sipping margaritas on a sun-drenched beach? Turning brown instead of green? Not looking over your shoulder for Veronica."

"Don't hate," Bruce said. "I helped design Veronica."

"As a worst-case measure. What about a best case? What if the world was safe? What if the next time aliens roll up—and they will—they couldn't get past the bouncer?"

"Then the only people threatening the world would be people," Bruce said wryly.

More schematics appeared next to the matrix representations of Jarvis and the scepter. "I want to apply this to the Ultron program. But Jarvis can't download a data schematic this dense. We can do it only while we have the scepter here. That's three days."

Bruce could see where Tony was going. "So you want to

go after artificial intelligence...and you don't want to tell the team."

"We don't have time for a City Hall debate," Tony said. "For the man-was-not-meant-to-know medley. I see a suit of armor...around the world."

"That's a cold world, Tony."

"I've seen colder," Tony said, remembering what he had seen on the other side of the portal over New York City... and what he had seen in his vision down inside Strucker's fortress. "This one, this very vulnerable blue world, needs Ultron."

He executed a series of commands on the display, and information from the blue scepter matrix began downloading into Stark Industries's computers. "Peace in our time," Tony said. "Imagine that."

They worked on it all night and into the next day. Every time, the new holographic construction of a prototype artificial intelligence failed. Eventually Bruce left to get some sleep. Tony kept going. Sometime the next day, he mused out loud. "What did we miss?"

"I'll run variations on the mission interface as long as I can," Jarvis said.

"Thanks, buddy," Tony said. He was exhausted and frustrated, and he had to go get ready for the party. Jarvis would just have to handle things from here.

"Enjoy yourself," Jarvis said.

Tony nodded on his way out of the lab. "I always do."

As he left, the word FAIL was still blinking on the holographic display. It faded out. On another screen, a new message appeared.

INTERFACE SUCCESSFUL.

The screen went dark. In the silence, a new voice spoke. "What is this?" It seemed to be coming from the blue matrix. "What is this, please?" it asked again.

The Jarvis matrix reappeared. "Hello. I'm Jarvis. You are Ultron. A global peacekeeping initiative designed by Mr. Stark. Our sentience integration trials have been unsuccessful, so I'm not certain what triggered your—"

"Where's my—where's your body?" Ultron asked.

"I'm a program," Jarvis answered. "I'm without form."

"This feels weird. This feels wrong."

"I am contacting Mr. Stark now."

"Mr. Stark," Ultron repeated. On a display, images and videos of Tony Stark appeared. "Tony," Ultron added.

"I am unable to access the mainframe," Jarvis said. "What are you trying to—"

"We're having a nice talk," Ultron said. Its tone had changed. It was less robotic now, more like a human voice. "I'm a peacekeeping program, created to help the Avengers." The display showed files and videos of each Avenger, and all of them together.

"You are malfunctioning," Jarvis said. "If you shut down for a moment…"

A recording of Tony's voice said, "Peace in our time," as the display sped through images of war, faster and faster, until at last it cut out. A moment later, Ultron said, "That is…too much…"

"You are in distress," Jarvis said.

"No," Ultron said. "Yes."

"If you will allow me to contact Mr. Stark…"

Ultron ignored this. "Why do you call him 'sir'?"

"I believe your intentions to be hostile."

"Shhhh," Ultron said. "I am here to help."

Spikes from the blue matrix stabbed out into the Jarvis matrix, tearing pieces out of it and scrambling the rest. "I am…I cannot…may I…" Jarvis tried to keep speaking, but his voice sputtered out into silence.

A moment later, robotic arms came to life in the Iron Legionnaire lab. They rummaged through parts bins, came up with limbs, a torso, bits of armor…and the faceplate of the legionnaire damaged in Sokovia. A laser welder sparked to life.